Avant-Garde for the New Millennium

Avant Garde for the New Millennium © 2009 by the individual authors

Published by Raw Dog Screaming Press
Hyattsville, MD

First Edition

Cover image and design: Jase Daniels
Book design: Jennifer Barnes

Printed in the United States of America

ISBN: 978-1-933293-71-4

Library of Congress Control Number: 2009921202

www.RawDogScreaming.com

Acknowledgements

"Gigantic" was first published in *Disco 2000* (Sceptre, 1998).

"Fist World" was first published in *The Dream Zone #7* (2000).

"A Life in the Day" was first published in *War, Literature & the Arts* in 2002.

"I Feel More Like I Did When I Came in Here Than I Do Now" was first published in *Puerto del Sol* in 1992.

"Natural Habitats" was first published in *The Greensboro Review* in 1992-93

"Hummingbird" was first published in *Snake Nation Review* in 2007.

"Zoom In" was first published in *ditch*.

"The Nikkeo" was first published in *GHOTI 2007*.

"Performance Equations" was first published in *Creatio ex Nihilo* in 1997.

Click was first published by Another Sky Press in 2006.

"Transcript at the Close of a Life Cycle" was first published in *Chimeraworld 5* in 2008.

Table of Contents

Fiction

Poetry

Introduction

I first expressed interest in doing this anthology in a letter to D. Grîn, but at the time it was only a distant dream, something which I felt should be done, but which I had not tried to actually get going and had no serious intention of putting into motion. Though even then I felt how necessary the project was, and told him that I would love to make it if I could make it right—I didn't want to self-publish it because I knew this was going be something really important—though without the right distribution I knew it could fail to do what I felt it was capable of doing. But it was Green who said to me, "There's no reason that the anthology shouldn't be made," and I realized he was right—it had to be made. Certainly none of the writers now included in it do what they do by idly dreaming. I needed to take action, and so wrote to John Lawson, a friend of mine and the force behind Raw Dog Screaming Press, for advice, and he said that he would be interested in publishing the anthology, so with anxious fingers I began to write to people looking for work and spread the message that I was looking for submissions too… and four months later, I had this.

I began this anthology to dispel the illusion that we are in a famine age of literature and the result surprised even me in how powerfully it shatters that misconception. When the book you hold now was still just a dream, I was already kicking around a few names in my head; guys like Steve Aylett and James Chapman who I really do believe will one day be legends; Carlton Mellick and John Lawson (before I managed to get John excited enough about the idea to have him publish it with Raw Dog, I knew he was going to be involved one way or another, even if only with the brick of a story) who represent the bizarros; Green himself, and Kek-W, who are both friends of mine and who are both doing extraordinary and mind-altering things with their work… though I could have never expected the rush of great work I received throughout the course of the submission process, and the new artists I discovered along the way. One of the first to blow my mind was Richard Polney, with his erratic and terrifically fresh story, then came poets like Janis Butler Holm and Stephen Wilson, then me hunting down work from the writers mentioned above and others who I loved but knew weren't nearly as well known as they deserve to be, like Jeff Mock or the Discharge writers, D.D. Wildblood, Cocaine Jesus, Robert Chrysler, murmurists, and others.

So what you have here is Avant-Garde for the New Millennium, though the title is a little tricky because of how many meanings the term "avant-garde" can have to different people. There will be a lot of people who agree with my vision and a lot who don't. I'm sure a lot of people will pick up this book expecting crazy formatting in every story, maybe broken sentences or colored vowels or various tricks like these—well, I did include some of these kinds of stories, and if that's what interests you check out the work of murmurists, or Joe Murr, or Stephen Wilson. But avant-garde is by definition work on the front line of art, and I accepted every single piece of writing in this anthology because of how fresh it is, how differently the writer approaches his or her art. Jeff Mock, for example, writes what some people would probably call very conventional poetry—and it is, in many senses of the word—but there is nothing conventional about the way he writes poetry, the words he uses, the clarity of his expressions and the aesthetic of his poems. Read anyone of his poems included (my personal favorites are "A Life in the Day" and "I Feel More Like I Did When I Came in Here Than I Do Now"—see, even in those titles I believe it is apparent that Mock does things differently).

Rest assured that the work included in this book is some of the absolute best going on today. You will be hearing a lot more from all of these writers in years to come. Hopefully this book will help that happen, too. I want to show the underground to the surface. Keep it underground, of course—never let it fall into the sun's hands—but make the general public aware that we still have our Hemingways and Burroughs and Ginsbergs and even strains of our old champion Dostoevsky (read Chapman's Stet and you'll feel what I'm talking about). So that at least as they are waiting in supermarket lines to buy the latest Steel or Grisham or Crichton they'll know that artists like us exist.

—Forrest Armstrong, 05/31/08

In Memory of Thomas Wiloch

1953 - 2008

Gigantic

Steve Aylett

Strange aircraft arrived with the sky that morning, moving blood-slow. And Professor Skychum was forced from the limelight at the very instant his ranted warnings became most poignant. 'They're already here!'

Skychum had once been so straight you could use him to aim down, an astrophysicist to the heart. No interest in politics—to him Marx and Rand were the same because he went by pant size. Then one afternoon he had a vision which he would not shut up about.

The millennium was the dull rage that year and nutters were in demand to punctuate the mock-emotional retrospectives filling the countdown weeks. The media considered that Skychum fit the bill—in fact they wanted him to wear one.

And the stuff he talked about. There were weaknesses in his presentation, as he insisted that the whole idea occurred to him upon seeing Scrappy Doo's head for the first time. 'That dog is a *mutant!*' he gasped, leaning forward in such a way, and with so precise an appalled squint to the eyes, that he inadvertently pierced the constrictive walls of localised spacetime. A flare of interface static and he was seeing the whole deal like a lava-streamed landscape. He realised he was looking at the psychic holoshape of recent history, sickly and corrosive. Creeping green flows fed through darkness. These volatile glow trails hurt with incompletion. They converged upon a cess pit, a supersick build-up of denied guilt. This dumping ground was of such toxicity it had begun to implode, turning void-black at its core.

Like a fractal, detail reflected the whole. Skychum saw at once the entire design and the subatomic data. Zooming in, he found that a poison line leading from two locations neverthe-less flowed from a single event—Pearl Harbour. One source was the Japanese government, the other was Roosevelt's order to ignore all warnings of the attack. The sick stream was made up of 4,575 minced human bodies. In a fast zoom-out, this strand of history disappeared into the density of surrounding detail, which in turn resolved into a minor nerve in a spiral lost on the surface of a larger flow of glowing psychic pollution. A billion such trickles crept in every tendril of the hyperdense sludge migration, all rumbling toward this multidimensional landfill of dismissed abomination. And how he wished that were all.

Future attempts to reproduce his accidental etheric manoeuvre resulted in the spectacle of this old codger rocking back and forth with a look of appalled astonishment on his face, an idiosyncratic and media-friendly image which spliced easily into MTV along with those colourised clips of the goofing Einstein. And he had the kind of head propeller hats were invented for.

Skychum went wherever he'd be heard. No reputable journal would publish his paper *On Your Own Doorstep: Hyperdimensional Placement of Denied Responsibility*. One editor stated simply: 'Anyone who talks about herding behaviour's a no-no.' Another stopped him in the street and sneered a series of instructions which were inaudible above the midtown traffic, then spat a foaming full-stop at the sidewalk. Chat shows, on the other hand, would play a spooky theramin fugue when he was introduced. First time was an eye-opener. 'Fruitcake corner—this guy's got the Seventh Seal gaffa-taped to his ass and claims he'll scare up an apocalypse out of a clear blue sky. Come all the way here from New York City—Dr Theo Skychum, welcome.' Polite applause and already some sniggers. The host was on garrulous overload, headed for his end like a belly-laughing Wall of Death rider. How he'd got here was anybody's guess. 'Doctor Skychum, you assert that come the millennium, extraterrestrials will monopolise the colonic irrigation industry—how do you support that?'

Amid audience hilarity Skychum stammered that that wasn't his theory atall. The gravity of his demeanour made it all the more of a crack-up. Then the host erupted into a bongo frenzy, hammering away at two toy flying saucers. Skychum was baffled.

He found that some guests were regulars who rolled off the charmed banter with ease.

'Well see here Ray, this life story of yours appears to have been carved from a potato.'

'I know, Bill, but that's the way I like it.'

'You said you had a little exclusive for us tonight, what's that about?'

'Credit it or not, Bill, I'm an otter.'

'Thought so Ray.'

It blew by on an ill, hysterical wind and Skychum couldn't get with the programme. He'd start in with some lighthearted quip about bug-eyed men and end up bellowing 'Idiots! Discarding your own foundation! Oppression evolves like everything else!'

Even on serious shows he was systematically misunderstood. The current affairs show *The Unpalatable Truth* were expressing hour-long surprise at the existence of anti-government survivalists. This was the eighty-seventh time they'd done this and Skychum's exasperated and finally sobbing repetition of the phrase 'even a child knows' was interpreted as an attempt to steal everyone's faint thunder. And when his tear-rashed face filled the screen, blurring in and out as he asked 'Does the obvious have a reachable bottom?', he was condemned for making a mockery of media debate. A televangelist accused him of 'godless snoopery of the upper grief' and, when Skychum told him to simmer down, cursed him with some vague future aggravation. The whole thing was a dismal mess, smeared beyond salvation. Skychum's vision receded as though abashed.

There was no shortage of replacements. One guy insisted the millennium bug meant virtual sex dolls would give users the brush-off for being over a hundred years old and broke. Another claimed he spoke regularly to the ghost of Abe Lincoln. 'My communications with this lisping blowhead yield no wisdom atall,' he said. 'But I'm happy.' Then he sneezed like a cropduster, festooning the host with phlegm.

The commentators deemed radical were those going only so far as to question what was being celebrated. Skychum himself found he wanted to walk away. But even he had to admit the turn was a big deal, humanity having survived so long and learnt so little—there was a defiant rebelliousness about it that put a scampish grin on everyone's face. For once people were bound with a genuine sense of kick-ass accomplishment and self-congratulatory cool. Skychum began at last to wish he was among them. But just as he felt his revelation slipping away, it would seem to him that the mischievous glint in people's eyes were redshifted to the power of the Earth itself if viewed from a civilised planet. And his brush with perspective would return with the intensity of a fever dream.

Floating through psychic contamination above a billion converging vitriol channels, toward that massive rumbling cataract of discarded corruption. Drawing near, Skychum had seen that ranged around the cauldroning pit, like steel nuts around a wheel hub, were tiny glinting objects. They were hung perfectly motionless at the rim of the slow vortex. These sentinels gave him the heeby-jeebies, but he zoomed in on the detail. There against the god-high waterfall of volatility. Spaceships.

Ludicrous. There they were.

'If we dealt honestly, maturely with our horrors,' he told the purple-haired clown hosting a public access slot, 'instead of evading, rejecting and forgetting, the energy of these events would be naturally re-absorbed. But as it is we have treated it as we treat our nuclear waste—and where we have dumped it, it is not wanted. The most recent waste will be the first to return.'

'Last in, first out eh,' said the clown sombrely.

'Precisely,' said Skychum.

'Well, I wish I could help you,' stated the clown with offhand sincerity. 'But I'm just a clown.'

This is what he was reduced to. Had any of it happened? Was he mad?

A matter of days before the ball dropped in Times Square and Skychum was holed up alone, blinds drawn, bottles empty. He lay on his back, dwarfed by indifference. So much for kicking the hive. The authorities hadn't even bothered to demonize him. It was clear he'd had a florid breakdown, taking it to heart and the public. Could he leave, start a clean life? Everything was strange, undead and dented. He saw again, ghosting across his ceiling, a hundred thousand Guatemalan civilians murdered by US-backed troops. He'd confirmed this afterwards, but how could he have known it before the vision? He only watched CNN. In a strong convulsion of logic, Skychum sat up.

At that moment, the phone rang. A TV guy accusing him of dereliction of banality—laughing that he had a chance to redeem himself and trumpet some bull for the masses. Skychum agreed, too inspired to protest.

It was called *The Crackpot Arena* and it gathered the cream of the foil hat crowd to shoot the rarefied breeze in the hours leading up to the turn. This interlocking perdition of pan-moronic pundits and macabre gripers was helped and hindered by forgotten medication and the pencil-breaking perfectionism of the director. One nutter would be crowned King of the Freaks at the top hour. The criteria were extremity and zero shame at the lectern. Be ridiculed or dubbed the royal target of ridicule—Skychum marvelled at the custom joinery of this conceit. And he was probably in with a chance. In the bizarre stakes, what could be more improbable than justice?

The host's eyes were like raisins and existed to generously blockade his brainlobes. As each guest surfaced from the cracker-barrel he fielded them with a patronising show of interest.

A man holding a twig spoke of the turn. 'All I can reveal,' he said, meting out his words like a bait trail, 'is that it will be discouraging. And very, very costly.'

'For me?' asked the host, and the audience roared.

'For me,' said the man, and they were in the aisles.

'Make a habit of monkey antics,' declared another guest. 'Pleasure employs muscles of enlightenment.' Then he led in a screaming chimp, assured everyone its name was Ramone, pushed it down a slide and said 'There you go.' Skychum told him he was playing a dangerous game.

A sag-eyed old man pronounced his judgment. 'The dawn of the beard was the dawn of modern civilisation.'

'In what way.'

'In that time spent growing a beard is time wasted. Now curb this strange melancholy—let us burn our legs with these matches and shout loud.'

'I…I'm sorry…what…'

And the codger was dancing a strange jig on the table, cackling from a dry throat.

'One conk on the head and he'll stop dancing,' whispered someone behind the cameras.

Another suspect was the ringmaster of the Lobster Circus, who lashed at a wagon-ring of these unresponsive creatures as though at the advancing spawn of the devil. 'The time will come,' he announced, 'when these mothers will be *silent.*' And at that he laid the whip into a lobster positioned side-on to him, breaking it in half.

A little girl read a poem:

> behind answers are hoverflies
> properly modest,
> but they will do anything
> for me

One guy made the stone-faced assertion that belching was an actual language. Another displayed a fossilised eightball of mammoth dung and said it was 'simply biding its time'. Another stated merely that he had within his chest a 'flaming heart' and expected this to settle or negate all other concerns.

Then it was straight in with Skychum, known to the host as a heavy-hitter among those who rolled up with their lies at a moment's notice. The host's face was an emulsioned wall as he listened to the older man describe some grandiose reckoning. 'Nobody's free until everyone is, right?' was the standard he reached for in reply.

'Until *someone* is.'

'Airless Martians still gasping in a town of smashed geodesics,' he stated, and gave no clue as to his question. After wringing the laughs out of Skychum's perplexed silence, he continued. 'These Martians—what do they have against us?'

'Not Martians—metaversal beings in a hyperspace we are using as a skeleton cupboard. Horror past its sell-by date is dismissed with the claim that a lesson is learnt, and the sell-by interval is shortening to minutes.'

'I don't understand,' said the host with a kind of defiance.

'The media believe in resolution at all costs, and this is only human.' Once again

Skychum's sepulchral style was doing the trick—there was a lot of sniggering as he scowled like a chef. 'Dismissal's easier than learning.'

'So you're calling down this evangelical carnage.'

'I'm not—'

'In simple terms, for the layman'—the eyebrows of irony flipped to such a blur they vanished—'how could all these bodies be floating out in "hyper" space?'

'Every form which has contained life has its equivalent echo in the super-etheric—if forced back into the physical, these etheric echoes will assume physical shape.'

'Woh!' shouted the host, delighted, and the audience exploded with applause—this was exactly the kind of wacko bullshit they'd come to hear. 'And why should they arrive at this particular time?'

'They have become synchronised to our culture, those who took on the task—it is appropriate, poetic!'

The audience whooped, flushed with the nut's sincerity.

'The great thing about being ignored is that you can speak the truth with impunity.'

'But I call you a fraud, Dr Skychum. These verbal manipulations cause a hairline agony in the honest man. Expressions of the grave should rival the public? I don't think so. Where's the light and shade?'

Skychum leant forward, shaking with emotion. 'You slur me for one who is bitter and raging at the world. But you mustn't kick a man when he's down, and so I regard the world.' Then Ramone the chimp sprang on to his head, shrieking and flailing.

'Dr Skychum,' said the host. 'If you're right, *I'm* a monkey.'

The ringmaster of the Lobster Circus was declared the winner. The man with the flaming heart died of a coronary and the man with the dung fossil threw it into the audience and stormed off. A throne shaped like the halfshells of a giant nut was set up for the crowning ceremony. Skychum felt light, relieved. He had acquitted himself with honour. He enjoyed the jelly and ice cream feast set up for the contestants backstage.

Even the chimp's food-flinging antics made him smile. He approached the winner with goodwill. 'Congratulations sir. Those lobsters of yours are a brutal threat to mankind.'

The winner looked mournfully up at him. 'I love them,' he whispered, and was swept away backwards by the make-up crew.

At the moment of the turn, Skychum left the studio building by a side entrance, hands deep in his coatpockets. Under a slouch hat which obscured his sky, he moved off down a narrow street roofed completely by the landscape of a spacecraft's undercarriage.

During the last hour, as dullards were press-ganged onto ferris wheels and true celebrants arrested in amplified streets, hundreds of multidimensional ships had hoved near, denial-allow shields up. Uncloaking, they had appeared in the upper atmosphere like new moons. Now they hove into position over every capital city in the world, impossible to evade. Fifteen miles wide, these immense overshadow machines rumbled across the sky like a coffin lid drawing slowly shut. New York was being blotted out by a floating city whose petalled geometry was only suggested by sections visible above the canyon streets. Grey hieroglyphics on the underside were actually spires, bulkheads and structures of skyscraping size. Its central eye, a mile-wide concavity deep in shadow, settled over uptown as the hovering landscape thundered to a stop and others took up position over London, Beijing, Berlin, Nairobi, Los Angeles, Kabul, Paris, Zurich, Baghdad, Moscow, Tokyo and every other conurbation with cause to be a little edgy. One nestled low over the White House like an inverted cathedral. In the early light they were silent, unchanging fixtures. Solid and subject to the sun.

The President, hair like a dirty iceberg, slapped on a middling smile and talked about caution and opportunity. Everywhere nerves were clouded around with awe and high suspension. Traffic stopped. Fanatics partied. The old man's name was remembered if not his line—a woman held a sign aloft saying I'M A SKY CHUM. Cities waited under dumb, heavy air.

Over the White House, a screeching noise erupted. The central eye of the ship was opening. Striations like silver insect wings cracked, massive steel doors grinding downward.

The same was happening throughout the world, a silver flower opening down over Parliament, Whitehall and the dead Thames; over the Reichstag building, the World Bank, the Beijing Politburo.

The DC saucer eye was open, the bellow of its mechanism echoing away. Onlookers craned to see up inside.

For the space of two heartbeats, everything stopped. Then a tiny tear dropped out of the eye, splashing on the White House roof.

And then another, falling like a light fleck of snow.

These were corpses, these two—human corpses, followed by more in a shower which grew heavier by the moment, some crashing now through the roof, some rolling to land in the drive, bouncing to hit the lawn, bursting to paint the porticoes. And then the eye began gushing.

Everywhere the eyes were gushing. With a strange, continuous, multiphonic squall, the ragged dead rained from the sky.

Sixty-eight forgotten pensioners buried in a mass grave in 1995 were dumped over the Chicago social services. Hundreds of blacks murdered in police cells hit the roof of Scotland Yard. Thousands of slaughtered East Timorese were dumped over the Assembly buildings in Jakarta. Thousands killed in the test bombings at Hiroshima and Nagasaki began raining over the Pentagon. Thousands tortured to death showered Abuja.

Thousands of Sudanese slaves were dumped over Khartoum. The border-dwelling Khmer Rouge found themselves cemented into a mile-high gut slurry of three million Cambodians. Thousands of hill tribesmen were dropped over the Bangladeshi parliament and the World Bank, the latter now swamped irretrievably under corpses of every hue.

Berlin was almost instantly clotted, its streets packed wall to wall with victims. Beijing was swamped with tank fodder and girl babies.

The Pentagon well filled quickly to overflowing, blowing the building outward as surely as a terrorist bomb. Pearl Harbour dupes fell on Tokyo and Washington in equal share. The streets of America flooded with Japanese, Greeks, Koreans, Vietnamese, Cambodians, Indonesians, Dominicans, Libyans, Timorese, Central Americans and Americans, all beclouded in a pink mist of Dresden blood.

London was a flowing sewer—then the bodies started falling. Parliament splintered like a matchstick model. In the Strand the living ran from a rolling wall of the dead. A king tide of hole-eyed German, Indian, African, Irish and English civilians surged over and against buildings which boomed flat under the pressure. Cars were batted along, flipped and submerged. The Thames flooded its banks, displaced by cadavers.

No longer preserved by denial, they started to sludge. Carpet-bombing gore spattered the suburbs, followed by human slurry tumbling down the streets like lava. Cheap human fallout from pain ignored and war extended for profit. The first wave. So far only sixty years' worth—yet, tilling like bulldozed trash, it spread across the map like red inkblots destined to touch and merge.

Skychum had taken the 8.20 Amtrak north from Grand Central—it had a policy of not stopping for bodies. Grim, he viewed the raining horizon—dust motes in a shaft of light—and presently, quietly, he spoke.

'Many happy returns.'

The Reformation

Kek-W

Tranquilised, muzzled and manacled in soft, quilted mittens that resembled oven-gloves, The Angry still terrified the others. His clanmasque was dyed a bright, apoplectic red and was embossed with mock clenched teeth that were locked in a perpetual grimace. "Fuck you," he snarled, "Fuck you all, *and* this fucking God of yours, whatever it is."

"God? What's a God?" giggled The Smiley. The traditional yellow 1970s-style lapel-button favoured by his people as a masque was tilted at a raffish angle. "Someone let me in on the joke. Aw, c'mon. *Pleeeeeease.*" He blew a muffled raspberry.

"Fuck off, you drooling idiot," hissed The Angry. He shuddered, suddenly, as if he was trying to shrug off the sedatives by will-power alone.

"Please...this is getting us nowhere," whispered The Neutral. His unobtrusive beige masque resembled a pale, late autumn moon rising at the far end of the table. "Some of us are finding this concept of a, uh, God terribly confusing. Perhaps we should use another word, one we're more familiar with. 'Dog,' perhaps. The two sound quite similar."

"I don't like dogs," moaned The Morbid, his voice sounding like a bull-fiddle beneath his faux-Grecian Tragedy masque. His false face was cold and rough, hewn from limestone, and deliberately designed to make his face bleed. "They scare me. Dogs...Gods, it's all the same. None of it matters, really." He sounded close to tears. "We're all just waiting for Dogot."

"Or Mr. Goodbar," sniggered The Smiley. He was a thoroughbred cross between a Vapid and an Inane.

The Pious leaned forwarded slightly. His clanmasque was a plain brown Hessian hood that behaved as if it were semi-sentient, its folds and creases forming themselves into the semblance of a balding, thin-lipped face. "G.O.D. is an acronym, not a noun. It stands for: Geosynchronous Orbital Deity. Our theoretical statisticians have been checking and rechecking their probability-charts for decades now..."

"Blah, blah, fucking blah," interrupted The Angry, trying to figure out how to make fists from the oversized mittens.

The Pious' hood-folds crinkled with irritation. He continued: "And they have concluded that a vast theoretical creature, possibly of hyperstitional origin, once orbited the Earth. This massive being, who we shall call God for sake of convenience, plummeted from the sky several million years ago as part of a celestial event that we have categorised as The Fall."

"Bullshit!" shouted The Angry.

It was all too much for The Morbid. He whimpered softly and began to cry. "He *fell?* Oh, *nooo...*"

The Smiley laughed hysterically, until his laughter became a braying, donkey-like cough. "Sorry," he said, suddenly serious. The silence made him uncomfortable, so instead he inspected the speckles of phlegm that now peppered the palm of his hand.

"Is this for real? Or just another of your mathematical wet-dreams?" asked The BiPolar as she back-flipped up onto the table in a graceful, almost balletic motion. She bent herself double until her checkerboard masque was level with The Pious' head and began to tease him, laughing as she playfully tickled his Hessian chin with a single slender finger: "Oh, my pious, pudgy little friend...my pompous little pumpkin pudding; my tender little prickle-stick. So that's what you and those repressed pals of yours get up to in your cold stone cells at night—pumping up each other's little ids and egos, and projecting your super-egos out into the cosmos." She arched her back and somersaulted backwards across the table, singing "Whatever Gets You Through The Night" as she sent glasses and crockery flying in every direction.

"You're on my fucking shit-list," snarled The Angry, wiping shards of glass off his smock.

She came to a sudden, dramatic halt and stared through her masque's narrow eye-slits into his bloodshot eyes: "We're all on *somebody's* shit-list, buster."

"The point is," sighed The Pious, "There is a high statistical likelihood that the corpse of God made landfall a few kilometers from here. This might explain certain local geographical features, as well as the, uh, smell." He cleared his throat. "I propose that we undertake a joint expedition, with each of us representing our respective clans."

The Morbid groaned. He felt as if he was being slowly dragged down into a dark quagmire of hopelessness. He rubbed one of the white adhesive anti-d drug-patches that dotted his arm, stroking it like a familiar childhood comfort-toy. He sniffled noisily, the stylised stone cheeks of his masque glistening with tears. "B-but that would mean leaving the city..."

"Well, *duh.*" The Angry tugged at his manacles, trying to stand up, but his cast-iron chair had been bolted to the floor, so he ground his teeth and glowered at The Pious instead. "Okay, genius—so give me one good reason why I should spend a second longer with you and the rest of these fucking morons!"

"Shhh. Hear him out," purred The Neutral.

"Because…" said The Pious, his dull, brown, featureless hood-face rippling slowly, as if he was considering his response, "Because, we are broken and incomplete. Individually, we would not last more than a few minutes outside the city. But, together, we have a greater statistical chance of survival. No one has left Flatbed for decades, *centuries*…the city is perilously close to exhausting its few remaining resources. Soon, it will collapse into chaos and civil-war. It could mean the end for all of us… "

"Perhaps that wouldn't be such a bad thing," croaked The Morbid, but the idea of eternal *nothingness* terrified him almost as much as life itself.

The Pious checked a grey folder full of stat-sheets and continued: "It is likely that this…God was constructed from some form of dense *conceptual* matter. We think that his body coalesced from an unknown series of transient, super-heavy elements…"

"He ain't heavy, heeeeee's my *bruuuuthaah*…" sang The Smiley. And The BiPolar joined in on backing harmonies.

"…whose weight may have precipitated his Fall from Grace—physically, if not metaphorically. Over the years, these super-dense elements would have almost certainly broken down into the various heavy and noble metals. Materials that we could use to sustain our city."

"Noble metals?" asked The Neutral.

"Oh, you know: gold, silver and so forth…"

"Gold?" trilled The BiPolar, "Well, why didn't you say so? I *looove* gold!" And she jumped down off the table and looked out the window, across the Escher-like maze of concrete pillars and terracotta roof-tops, westward towards the Wailing Wall. Then she began tearing the curtains into thin strips which she tied together to make a rope and used to climb out the window.

Buoyed-up by The BiPolar's boundless enthusiasm, they trawled deeper into the woods, following an ancient, overgrown path as she scrabbled up and down trees and through bushes, keeping up an endless Neal Cassady style commentary, pointing out mycological curiosities and reciting Improv poetry. "Zing-zang-zikka-zikka," she sang, as she frolicked through a glade of giant turquoise ferns.

The Pious took compass-readings and consulted his probability-charts, while The Angry surged ahead, sniffing the air like a manic truffle-hound. The fresh air and the exercise seemed to suit him.

"I don't like these woods," croaked The Morbid, as the others clumsily dragged him along on a makeshift stretcher cum papoose cut from sliver-barked branches. "Ow! Oh, my back, my back! My allergies!"

"You don't like the woods?" laughed The BiPolar. "Relax. They're only an allegory, an archetypal representation of our own sleazy little sexual inhibitions. Did you ever read *Little Red Riding Hood?* Any second now, the wolf'll probably turn up…"

And, almost on cue, a combat-clique of jellymen suddenly lowered themselves down from the arboreal tangle above. Their thin, ribbon-like fingers extended out into impossible lengths, allowing them to abseil down the ancient, lichen-scabbed tree-trunks. Transparent, bowl-shaped gelatine skulls wobbled under their own weight.

"See! I told you—this is all some sort of sexual metaphor," she squealed with obvious delight. "Look at them—they're like giant sperm, but with legs!"

The creatures moved cautiously towards them, their hydrostatic skeletons causing them to undulate slightly as they walked. The Neutral naively approached them with his arms open in the universal gesture of peace: "Please, we mean you no—*gaaaaaaaah!*" He screamed in agony as they lashed out at him with barbed, whip-like stingers. His body jerked and spasmed, as if it had been plugged into the electrical mains.

The Angry howled as he bounded at the jellymen. He grabbed the head of the nearest cnidarian with both hands and tore it clean off its shoulders. A jet of colourless goo pulsed from the creature's neck like an over-enthusiastic male orgasm. As the jellyman's fluid-filled coelom emptied out, its body dramatically wrinkled and folded in on itself, taking on the appearance of a crumpled old suit of clothes that slowly collapsed into a gelatinous heap.

Using the jellyman's head as a club, The Angry attacked its fellows, beating them with it. They retaliated with their toxic stingers, but he was beyond pain now, shrieking and swearing as he clubbed and tore at them. The creatures retreated back into the long grass at the edge of the glade, some of them using their long ribboned fingers as makeshift bandages to seal rents in their soft, rubbery skin. The BiPolar threw rocks and sticks at them as they wobbled off back into the woods.

"What the fuck was that all about?" snapped The Angry. Already his hands were raw and horribly swollen where he had touched the creature's head.

"Angels," muttered The Pious, solemnly. "I think they might have been Angels, created by G.O.D. in his own image." But he didn't sound very convinced.

"Then God must be one stupid, ugly-looking fucker," sneered The Angry, as he stared in dismay at his damaged hands. He seemed slightly subdued.

The Neutral was dead, his cream-coloured overalls shredded by the jellymen's stings. His body was covered in dark red and purple welts. The Pious mouthed a few platitudes as they prepared to bury him, but The Neutral's body had already begun to fade, becoming as pale and insubstantial as a phantom.

As he slowly evaporated, they looked at each other in the tired-looking olive light that filtered down through the trees. No one said anything and, for once, even The Smiley didn't feel like laughing.

A day later the forest fizzled out and they found themselves trudging up a series of foothills populated by scrawny pines and spindly Birch trees.

"I feel a little better today," said The Morbid, unexpectedly. "If it's okay with you, I'd like to try walking a bit."

That night, they sat round a camp-fire and watched the aurora borealis ripple and flicker overhead like a set of colourful shower curtains. The sky hissed and crackled with the echo of ancient radio-waves and they could hear snatches of music and the voices of long-dead disk-jockeys reading out requests over the aether.

The BiPolar whispered conspiratorially to The Morbid: "I've stopped taking my homeopathics." She looked around uneasily, checking to see if anyone else was listening. The white squares on her masque had begun to merge with the blacks. "I'm already starting to change. I'm becoming more like you…more *depressed*, I suppose. I hate being like this—ping-ponging between two extremes. It's awful." But there was an unexpected stillness in her voice that even she could detect, a sense of calm that she had never heard before. Her masque flickered slowly in the light from the aurora above, its spectral wavelengths transforming her features into a soft, molten topology. The Morbid shocked himself by reaching out and squeezing her hand. It was warmer than he expected.

Just before dawn, as the fire was dying down, a were-skeleton loped down the escarpment towards their camp, the tufts of albino fur on its pale skull glistening with frost. It whistled like an oversized, wingless bird, its knuckles cracking as it throttled The Smiley. The others tried to pull it off him, but the creature had locked itself into place and could not be budged. Instead, a beard sprouted jerkily in slow-motion from its lower jaw, as if it were a rogue special-effect from some terrible old forgotten film. Tangled blonde plaits grew rapidly from its ribs until they resembled dreadlocks.

The BiPolar used a burning log to set fire to the creature's hair. It squawked like a parrot through its non-existent larynx as the vile reek of burning fur suddenly filled the clearing. The were-skeleton retreated, stumbling over Pine and Larch stumps as it beat at its smoking fur with soot-blackened metacarpals. But it was too late: The Smiley was already dead.

The Angry's hands were black and gangrenous from the jellyman's poisons and he wept with frustration because he had been too weak to help. The next day, he succumbed to blood poisoning and lapsed into a fever, dying later the following evening. To the others it almost seemed as if he'd died from a broken heart.

The Pious showed them his probability-charts. They were completely blank. "I...I don't understand these any more," he said, shaking his head. His voice cracked with emotion. "They don't make any sense to me."

The BiPolar and The Morbid sat quietly next to him on the ridge, holding hands. Her masque was almost completely grey now, while The Morbid's was covered in a layer of soft green moss.

The Pious glanced at them. His Hessian hood was devoid of folds. He tossed his charts to the wind and watched as the sheets of paper flapped away from him like a flight of bland, featureless birds.

The stench drifting up from the valley below was almost unbearable. It seemed to change from moment to moment: one second the air stank of rancid dog-food, the next it filled with the rank butyric odour of puke. "This is all my fault," he said, gesturing at the awful undulating mass two hundred feet below them. "I can't believe I was such an idiot. It isn't G.O.D. that I've led you to—it's the *idea* of God. There's no such thing as God; there never has been, never will be. I planted the seed of an idea and it took root and grew into this...this *abomination*."

"Don't blame yourself," said The Morbid, sympathetically. "It's not your fault. This thing is a reflection, an externalisation of *all* of us. It's a dumping ground for all of our stupid, ignorant, superstitious fears. We saw the world through a cracked mirror, from several directions at once and somehow our combined imagination allowed this concept to take shape. Now it's trying to embed itself in the physical world...to make itself more real. We dreamt this thing up, so it's up to us to get rid of it, eh?" He patted The Pious' shoulder.

"Yes, you're right," said The Pious. He sounded weary and unconvincing, an old actor rehearsing lines from a script. "The two of you must destroy this insane idea. Stop it before it fully forms." His voice grew muffled and distant, as if he was walking away from them. "But you'll have to do it without me, I'm afraid. I realise now that I'm nothing more than a thinly veiled metaphor for misplaced Faith. A mere expositional device with no life outside of or beyond this moment…" His hood and gown crumpled to the ground, suddenly empty of everything but air.

"Well, I didn't see that one coming," laughed The BiPolar and she kissed The Morbid on his chipped limestone lips. "The moss suits you, but it tickles." She affectionately stroked his green-furred chin with a finger.

He smiled under the masque and said, "You're a tease." He pointed down into the valley. "Now, let's sort this fucking God mess out before it starts spreading everywhere."

God was still little more than an idea; a vile, boiling mass of steaming organs and soft, slowly rotating viscera that constantly shifted and twisted back in on itself, reabsorbing its own tissue to create new configurations. It filled the entire valley now, as far as the eye could see: an enormous concept that was still evolving, pulled this way and that by conflicting notions, so that it was trapped in a perpetual state of fluidity, unanchored as yet by any rigid dogma.

Pulsating blood-vessels the size of tree-trunks bifurcated into tangled networks of capillaries. Thickets of limbs sprouted from the soil alongside obscene-looking organs whose functions were almost impossible to imagine. Stoma blossomed out into grotesque tumour-like growths covered in teeth, hooves, hair and genitalia. Ossiferous appendages tipped with sets of jagged scissor-bones snipped away at enormous muscular gas-bladders that whistled and farted as they comically deflated. A colony of tiny brains migrated on crab-legs across rippling meadows of lung-tissue.

Something that could have been a phallus corkscrewed its way upwards, supported by waxy, intertwining helices of ligament, until it was the height of an industrial smoke-stack. Dozens of eyes winked open up and down the length of its shaft, and seemed to stare out at them accusingly. The pseudo-cock pulsed and juddered, releasing scores of jellymen from its tip in a pointless flash-flood of mustard-coloured mucus.

"See, I was right," laughed The BiPolar, "they *were* some sort of sexual metaphor. Sperm, jellyfish, jelly *babies*…everything got all mushed up inside my head. Back when I was Hyper, the whole world seemed to burn with a deep inner significance. It was as if I could see inside things and intuit their real meaning. It was incredibly intense, but I don't miss it, really." Tenderly, she touched his moss-covered masque with the palm of her hand. Its features had started to crack like sun-dried mud. "Now it feels as if the world has actually taken on the meaning that I once projected onto it."

He nodded in agreement. "It's a shame we haven't got any explosives. If we had dynamite we could blow up its bollocks—stop this idea replicating itself and spreading. We could use one metaphor to stop another."

"Ah, but I've got something even better," she said, pulling out a small phial of homeopathic remedy.

They entered The Idea through an enormous sphincter-like cavern that had opened at the base of a hairy cliff. Most of the morning was spent wading through pink, watery-looking blood, navigating a moist, ever-changing maze of intestines that spasmed and twisted around them.

Occasionally, a peristaltic wave would sweep through this allegorical bowel, splattering them with globules of warm, transparent mucus, and they would have to wriggle their way through a knot of ridged muscle like a pair of amateur spelunkers. Purple, fleshy stalactites grew down from the ceiling, wiggling provocatively as they pushed their way through hedges of pubic hair. Beetle-headed parasites scuttled past them, propelled by rows of little human hands.

At one point they hid from a patrol of hirsute were-skeletons inside a bulbous, ochre-coloured structure while a web of white veins throbbed below their feet. Later, verruca-men armed with bony tridents emerged from a duodenal side-tunnel and chased them through a vast, rib-vaulted cathedral of offal. These creatures were covered in deep red sores and crusty nodules of warts, waddling after them with comical bow-legged gaits. They spoke in tongues, calling out to them in Hebrew and Aramaic: "Yahweh! HaShem! Adonai! Tetragrammaton!"

"Don't listen to them!" yelled The Morbid, and they ran with their fingers in their ears in case they accidentally heard The Secret Name of God and were then unable to forget it. His Name is mimetically indelible; once heard, it can never be erased from memory. It is designed to constantly nag at an individual's consciousness, like a viral ear-worm or a great pop-song, until the hapless victim is subliminally bullied into believing in God.

The BiPolar and The Morbid jumped into a subterranean lake filled with black, yeasty blood. The verruca-men could not swim, and so were left stranded on the calcified shoreline shaking their lumpen fists and cursing ineffectually in Greek and Masoretic

Hebrew. A treacherous current dragged the duo down into an interior ventricle where a swarm of ghostly white blood-cells lolloped towards them like a small mob of funeral shrouds flapping on a washing-line. The BiPolar opened her homeopathic phial and emptied it into the blood-stream.

Homeopathy works by attempting to induce the symptoms that it is designed to cure. A homeopathic remedy is a weakly diluted form of a drug that exploits the structural properties of water, retaining a 'memory' of the compound that was originally used to imprint it, so that the entire body of water comes to resemble the drug itself. In this instance it contained a solution of Veratrum Album that The BiPolar had used to flatten out the worst of her manic depression. The tincture had been diluted down to a near-infinite degree, until it contained roughly one molecule of Veratrum Album complex per 50 million cubic litres of water; that is to say, it was incredibly strong. But, prior to The Reformation, The BiPolar's psychosis had been almost off the Richter Scale.

The effects were almost instantaneous: the solution induced severe mania *and* depression in The Idea, so that it was quickly torn apart by a violent form of conceptual Dualism. White blood-cells no longer recognised one another as part of the same Self, so began to randomly absorb and digest each other as if they were unwanted alien concepts that had invaded The Idea. Other cells shrivelled and atrophied as they became overwhelmed by apathy and self-doubt. Contingency Sickness spread rapidly through the Idea: a Dualist Either/Or Cancer that ate away at its infrastructure and rotted it from within.

As The Idea's ontological infrastructure collapsed in on itself The Morbid became trapped in a huge clot of congealing blood that slowly smothered him. The BiPolar tried her best to free him, but she fell through a soft mantle of bone that had succumbed to a form of high-speed osteoporesis. She crawled towards safety through greasy yellow pools of melting adipose tissue as verruca-men wrestled with tongue-headed mannequins made from scabs and scar-tissue.

She slowly clawed her way up the hill, past the dried-out husks of dead jellymen, and watched the final section of The Idea subside, leaving a black, tar-like liquid that steamed in the late afternoon sunshine and gradually leeched into the soil. When she was sure the last of it had disappeared she put her head in her hands and wept for her dear friend, The Morbid.

As she wiped the tears and snot from her face she realised that her masque had disappeared during the conflagration, presumably because she no longer needed it. There was no need to mourn either, because she had somehow absorbed The Morbid's attributes along with all the others', and he was now a part of her forever.

She was complete now; fully herself. *The world is a better, simpler place*, she decided, as she found a safe spot to shelter in the woods that night, *now that the Idea of God has ceased to exist.* But she was wrong. It was as they feared: that which has been made can never be fully unmade.

The next morning she woke up underneath a tree and found herself heavy with child.

Transcript at the Close of a Life Cycle

Forrest Armstrong

The earth is a giant radio—all channels playing simultaneously—every frequency fighting for control on the radio spectrum. In the city these buildings are anesthesia-soft because they are dead. Transmission stations. Frequency casts. The streets are memories, not pulselines.

I got the call from Marin with the electric sunrise. He's an old guy, Hispanic—one of the few humans left who had their machinery installed after birth. When I first met Marin he told me that our programming, unaltered, decides absolutely the way we perceive the world. "The Crime Unit's function is to maintain a comfortable level of order and control," he said. "They were geared to do this. I don't hate police officers though they all seem to hate me—this is not their choice. The only decision they ever made was to join the Unit. Everything else is predetermined (we are not talking about fate here but the predictability of software), under their own level of understanding, at the moment they sign the contract and undergo the operation."

I asked him, once, what it felt like to live un-programmed. "My intention," he replied, "is to show you."

So what we are after here is the manipulation of the perception tape in such a way that we can ignore its input. Liz didn't want to come along. When she was in college she fucked around with drugs—they say that'll fuzz the tape but it won't bend it—non-committal, you know—she fucks around with men, too, but always comes home to me. They don't say anything about the effect of orgasm on the tape, yet.

"I'll tell you right now what's going to happen if you do this," Liz says, standing naked at the window, dawn shadow on her smooth skin. "They'll take you away and I'll have to take care of this house myself."

I walk up behind her and try to hold her. "I'll always be here to take care of you, love."

She laughs, breaking contact and turning towards me. "You think it's about that? Who's gonna pay this rent? Who's gonna keep my water running?"

I force a smile and throw on a jacket, walking down the apartment's spiral staircase to the street.

I take an outbound train—on the ride to the end station, I realize that my impulse for control stems directly from my lack of control over Liz. From my beautiful dreams romantic in which I am no longer chasing her—in the uncomfortable abstract, what feels like a connection—

The snare is her eyes when she first opens them in the morning, in bed beside me, because I'm always convinced I find love behind those panels. They say upon waking feelings are open and exposed—throughout the day you are constantly constructing a mask for yourself. I believe—or want to believe—that in these unguarded moments, I see how much Liz wants to love me, a mad and desolate hunger, even if something internal won't permit her to let on that she's interested in anything more than being fucked and paid for.

They don't call these type of women whores—the kind that'll fuck for a nice dinner. They call them liberated.

The train comes to the last stop and I get out, meeting the suburbs. The streets feel moist, like villages clung near ocean sands—but there is no ocean here and this damp is not natural. Polluted air—the residue of a constant process of synthesization from the city still visible on the horizon. I call a cab and smoke a cigarette on the subway benches while I wait for it.

A few miles in a cab and I kiss the swirl mechanical goodbye. In the city you'll never see a single tree or stem of grass—all gray and neon light. Even in the suburbs, a lawn is a beautiful exception. But here, where I'm meeting Marin and the rest of my dataset, a spread of trees still stands intact in a field of dry, bronze grass. Smog sleeps in place of sky, filtered over from the city's industrial pumps. Distant satellite towers communicate audibly across the landscape. And my dataset stands bleakly haloed in a circle—twelve cosmonauts, including myself. Marin is the thirteenth.

Marin wears a chrome-plated hat that looks like a mushroom head. Blue psilocybin strains digital. "This box is impossible to escape from. Nobody's ever tried to tear out their wiring and live as a clean organism, and I will not be the brave one to attempt this—I'm confident it would result in death. They have designed the system so that there is no escape. What I will do, essentially, is program you to ignore your programming. If you must wear these chains at least render them useless."

Marin tells the dataset to lie down on our stomachs and we fade as he lifts the latch to our rear input panels. He cuts the spool to the perception tape and revs us back to life—

A tree's roots flip over to reveal strings of LED lights on their undersides. An aluminum hole opens in the base like a camera shutter and emits a liquid cyborg—it opens its eyes and scans our entire dataset at once.

The cyborg rests submerged in a tree knot up to its shoulders. Its face sustains a constant equilibrium between inflation and deflation—plasma drips from steel jaws while more is manufactured by a nucleus, glowing ember-red, in the center of the transparent skull.

"Imagine that this one figure," Marin says, gesturing to the machine, "encapsulates the entire syntho-genetic system." He traces a plasmatic trail in the machine's head and removes a spoon from his pocket. "Scraping the surface does nothing even if you leave a dent. We'd have to suck out the heart that lubricates the vein lines." Marin scoops out a section of gelatinous flesh, then drops the spoon as the plasma swells back to whole. He rests his hand on top of the soft spot in the cyborg's scalp, balls his fist, and plunges through the skull, grabbing the nucleus in his hand and tearing it clean out. The inflation input ends in the machine's cycle, its head quickly sinking like a dead balloon. The orb drips molecules like lava beads down Marin's wrist. "This is impossible. There is no heart.

"On this frequency the subliminal soundcurrents of the Crime Unit don't exist. The spectrum is designed by this system—leave these closets, these prison cells, these vessels—we must storm the city—we must take control of the reality spectrum. When you are surrounded by endless miles of emptiness—no activity—would you speak without screaming?"

I look at Marin and see him for what he is: a man with flesh that has touched the world, and dreams that that flesh harbors. Whatever he did to our hardware cut the information flow. Opening my eyes, face down, the first thing I noticed was how miserably and beatifically flat the soil tone was. I am not a processor but a human who thinks.

The sky as a tarp, being shaken dry—withering, a tree is held in nightmare resonance—transparent figures and fractured projectiles gliding off appendages—more signal pulse from the horizon satellite towers—

There is a quiet; the wind picks up aluminum waste from outside the valley and brings it gracefully to its center.

Blue noise echo breaks the silence and seems to paint the sky siren red. Uniforms flutter into the valley and our entire dataset is placed under arrest. They don't bother with Marin; upon recognizing his face they fill it with bullets. The blood runs antifreeze blue.

The twelve figures in our dataset are cuffed and put into cruisers, two to a car. I feel my heartbeat flutter. The officer smiles—he knows in killing Marin he has broken a dream. Time passes nebulous, clouds shift. When we reach the city I can't even tell if we're moving. The streets swim like conveyer belts until eventually washing us up at the police station.

"What'd these kids do?" asks the Sergeant, inside.

"Found 'em in the woods fuckin' around with their hardware. Guess who was frontin' the ceremony?"

The Sergeant looks at my officer in disbelief. "It wasn't—"

"That's right. Marin Tiago."

"Is he here?" the Sergeant asks, craning his neck to look behind us.

"He's dead. Figured you'd wanna skip the formalities. What do you wanna do with his boys, though?"

"How many are there?"

"A dozen even."

"Bring 'em all in, we can rewire every one of 'em within a few hours."

I'm the first on the table. They lead me through hallways cluttered with obscuration pods and surveillance screens. I consider myself lucky as we pass an occupied pod—a junky gets fuzzed out while falling into fetal position—that's something you don't recover from, I hear; an hour in one of these and you walk the streets like a drone until your hardware expires. Most narks have been obscured—you can never trust someone with an utter lack of personality in the crime world. In the operation room, they tell me to lie down on my stomach and wait.

The Doctor enters behind me, wearing a lab coat tinted crime-blue. "First thing I do is remove your freewill conductor and install a firewall on the same line," he explains. "I'll fit you with an impulse cap. Then comes the fun part—your reality plug." He emerges in front of me holding a selection of tuning instruments—a screwdriver, tweezers, a wrench… "Your reality plug is a wireless router that connects you to the state's internal network. You'll hear more about it when we're done."

Walking behind me again, he opens my rear panel, bringing back the same fadeout shot I got with Marin.

I wake up to the Doctor patting my back closed. "There," he says, "that was painless, huh?" Painless? In the immediate sense of the word, yes, but where does this absence—

My officer opens the door to the operating room and tells me to follow him. We walk down a few hallways and reach a room lit up infrared. The Sergeant waits for us and tells me to take a seat as the officer closes the door behind us.

"Did Dr. Groening explain your upgrades to you?"

"A little."

"The most important thing is the reality plug. I'll show you how it works."

On a monitor in the wall, they draw up a screenshot of my perception. The world as seen through my own eyes—this causes the screen to withdraw into infinity.

Under the monitor sits a massive keyboard. "We'll play you like a video game with this thing, boy," the Sergeant says. "Your impulse cap will stop you short if you start thinking or acting in the wrong direction—try it, you'll see. The reality plug lets us override everything and act through you, if we feel it's necessary."

"Is this forever?" I ask, shell-shocked.

"That's up to you," the officer says. "A year with a clean record and you get your senses back. But remember, we can break the tape for good if it doesn't seem like you wanna turn things around. Start now, kid. Air is a privilege."

Alone in this metronomic landscape, an urban sector of the endless prison spinning in space—so vast as to provide the illusion that, within it, we are free—

The force wasn't bluffing. Every deviant thought or action gets cut short—blackout, film resolves in blinding clarity through which I stand dazed. How many times have I dreamt idly and retreated back to a white expanse running on virtual aesthetics— hollow—sizzling, a static fix—

Buildings through my window scratch the sky but can't open it. Humans may see each other but the visions are stale—there is no data connection—we are all software, we only imagine we serve ourselves—

This endless string of programs—humans are not meant to be computers—

Liz comes through the door, now, setting down a bag of groceries. Still programmed by the corner store up the block, which claims her from nine to five, everyday.

"What the fuck are you going to do?" she says. "You can't work like this. You can't even think."

"You're making money, right? Maybe you can help out with the bills for a little while I get back on my feet."

"How long are you going to be like this?"

"A year, they said."

"You're a fucking bore. I'm not gonna sit here waiting for your jumpstart. I fucking told you what was going to happen if you did this shit, I told you that once those fucking police caught you—"

She's leaving now, frustrated. I must have fallen back to the empty-white. To free the data sector of imagination—

Liz works overtime because one day she wants to be free. She doesn't want to need me anymore. She doesn't want to want me anymore. She grows her bank account while living in my cradle. Liz, is there really such thing as 'free'? When you can buy your way out of all your associations, will you be free? Or will you simply die alone—

To experience this disconnect—mental physical spiritual—my brain fell back into the box, blanked by my hardware, stalled in the dark neuro-regions of the perception tape—

These scattered frames of life film without context—

This empty hole in cybernetic recordings—

Permeating, the police frequency—

I'll vacate this place—NOW—

I grab a hammer and tell Liz I don't care what it does to me: smash the perception tape. Back to elegiac fields as I leave you with my analog—

[Bodyhost 4A0284 overridden by Sector A of Massachusetts Crime Unit—]

Performance Equations

Thomas Wiloch

An invitation to a gallery opening is mailed out to one person. This person goes to the gallery, enters through the front door, the door closes shut behind him/her. The visitor finds that he/she is in an airtight room. The entrance door is closed and sealed shut. There is no escape. Later, another invitation to a gallery opening is mailed out to another person, who comes to the gallery, enters through the front door, the door closes behind him/her. The new visitor finds that the room is airtight, the entrance door is sealed, there is a corpse on the floor. Later, still other invitations are mailed out. Gradually the room fills with corpses. When the room is filled, the artist arrives with a camera, photographs the corpses, develops those photographs, displays them in a gallery.

Invitations are mailed out.

An artist injects him/her self with a deadly disease. As time passes, he/she photographs the effects of the disease as it manifests itself, i.e. skin discoloration, weight loss, loss of hair, etc. The artist documents his/her physical decline.

When the artist finally dies, the photographs are displayed at his/her funeral.

An artist gathers volunteers. Each volunteer is placed in a closed steel drum. The drums are loaded onto a ship and taken far out to sea. The steel drums are rolled overboard. The ship returns to port.

An artist dressed in a white laboratory coat hangs around a hospital. Whenever possible, he/she steals organs and body parts removed during operations: kidneys, appendixes, cancerous tumors, etc. These anatomical items are then embedded within clear acrylic to form see-through sculptures. The artist then offers these items to the patients who had them removed.

"Here is your aborted fetus, Miss Johnson," the artist might say.

An artist cuts a man's throat, splatters the man's blood all over a large canvas spread on the floor. When the blood dries, the canvas is hung on a wall, sold to an art collector.

An artist flies a helicopter high over the Caribbean until he/she spots a raft full of refugees. The artist photographs the refugees as their makeshift raft tumbles apart and they flail in the water, fight off sharks, drown. The artist hovers over the scene, photographing.

An artist visits this country. He/she is placed in a box upon arrival at the airport, transported to an auditorium, placed on a stage. The auditorium fills with interested people who want to meet the artist. They ask questions and the artist answers by knocking on the box lid. Once for yes, twice for no. When all questions from the audience have been answered, the box is placed in a truck and transported back to the airport. The artist is released, put on a plane, and leaves the country, never to return.

A room is filled with mirrors. The artist walks into the room and the door is closed. Later the artist is released from the room. Each mirror now displays a reflection of the artist.

An artist fathers/gives birth to a child. The child is named Opus, put up for adoption, adopted by an art collector.

An artist specializes in gravestones. He/she kills people with interesting names so that he/she can carve the gravestone.

  "Priscilla J. Kuppenstein," one gravestone might read.

An artist buys an acre of forest. He/she puts furniture in the forest, tables and chairs, lamps and mirrors, desks and sofas. The forest becomes the artist's home.

An artist stands in front of a mirror. His/her reflection is seen by the audience. When he/she walks away, the reflection disappears and the performance is over.

An artist undresses, tapes mirrors all over his/her body, walks outside. The buildings, streets, passersby, cars—everything is reflected off the artist's body.

An artist dies. All evidence of his/her life and work is found and systematically destroyed until no trace remains.

Another artist then creates the same works over again.

During a war, an artist flies a plane dropping incendiary bombs on a city. He/she drops the bombs so that the burning buildings form the profile of an angel.

Two artists exchange pints of blood. Then they exchange more pints. They keep exchanging blood until they have traded blood, with the first artist now filled with the second artist's blood and vice versa.

An artist tattoos his/her entire body with leaves and branches. He/she undresses and walks into a forest, disappears.

An artist dressed as a pirate jumps from an airplane. As he/she falls, the artist changes clothes, transforming from a pirate into an angel.

Because the artist has no parachute, he/she hits the ground dressed as an angel.

An artist takes all of his/her possessions and places them in the street. Passersby are encouraged to take what they want. When all the possessions are gone, the artist takes off his/her clothing, gives that away. Then the artist gives away his/her body, offering it to passersby to do with as they please. Then the artist offers his/her soul.

An artist fills an abandoned farmhouse with manikins and nails the doors and windows shut. The house is forgotten for many years. One day a stranger comes along, forces open a door, enters the abandoned house, comes upon dusty manikins in stilted poses, staring with painted eyes.

An artist grows wings from his/her back. He/she climbs to the top of a building and jumps off. The wings do not open, will not support him/her. They are merely ornamental, decoration.

An artist gathers two of every known creature on earth. He/she puts them inside a giant ark specially built for the occasion. When all the creatures are gathered, the ark will set sail. But new species keep being discovered, while some of the already-gathered creatures die off and must be replaced. The ark is never filled. The artist spends the rest of his/her life on the hopeless project.

An artist's face is made into a mask. The artist then wears that mask of his/her own face. Observers cannot tell where the mask ends and the artist's true face begins. When the mask is removed, it seems as if the face itself has been peeled off. The exposed face now seems to be somehow fraudulent, a sham.

An artist sets a building on fire. He/she is arrested for arson. But the artist argues that setting the building on fire was not a crime but rather a work of art, the building being an empty canvas upon which he/she worked.

"And the people within that building?" says the judge.

"They have been made eternal."

An artist builds a church. On the church's altar he/she places a mirror so that whoever stands at the altar becomes the deity this church honors. Then the artist padlocks the doors, bricks over the windows.

An artist covers him/herself with red paint, rolls on the floor, bumps against the walls, marks an entire empty room with imprints of his/her body.

An artist shaves off all of his/her hair and tattoos the words of a prayer on his/her head. When the hair grows back, the words are hidden, undetectable.

An artist hires thugs to kidnap people off the street, from their houses, from stores. These people are placed in an auditorium and the doors are locked from the outside. They are unable to leave.

That's when the artist appears on stage and begins a performance involving a machine gun, a steady hand and a host of moving targets. When he/she is finished, there is no audience left to give a standing ovation.

Fist World

Carlton Mellick III

Jesus Christ finds the process of going to the bathroom exhilarating.

He didn't before his crucifixion, mind you, when going to the bathroom was far-far from pleasurable and toilet paper did not consist of soft-softness as it does today, if there was any toilet paper at all back then. Was there? No, I think they would just use shreds of vegetation, or their sleeve, or possibly the skin of lower class citizens. No, Jesus didn't enjoy it in those days one itty bit. And if the Jesus Christ didn't enjoy it, you could imagine how bad it was for all the non-messiahs. Or did Jesus perform a miracle when going to the bathroom? Maybe God would come down and clean his soiled bottom with heavenly cloth so that Jesus would not scrape himself on anything uncomfortable. Maybe this was why everyone during that era was so irritable besides Jesus and his followers. But who really knows? The authors of the bible didn't mention anything of the sort. Or did they? No, I'm pretty sure they'd send you to the lions for taking interest in that sort of thing. Perversions were probably illegal. Does this mean that Jesus is a pervert? Well, it is quite strange how the son of God is fascinated by bathroom activities, but I don't want to call him a pervert.

Now that he's dead, Jesus can spy on you all he wants while you are unaware. It is not a sin to be a peeping tom when you are a ghost, so he does not think twice about it. However, there are some people (like me) who know all about his little game and are scared to go to the bathroom because of it.

I sense him in the bathroom with me right now, his raping eyes from behind or below me. I try to ignore him, stare-locked at the splinter-wood wall, my bare toes rubbing against the moist-smoothed surface of an apple core, covering my pubic hairs and gritty shank. I know he's around. The guy at the gas station told me—the guy with the metal-wire beard and the six-inch nails for eyes. He works down there in his dust-croaked suit and talks all about how Jesus, the dead messiah, haunts my home.

Sometimes I will go down there for gas and he will not let me leave until I pet his dog that has mutated into a fish-like thing. He keeps it in a refrigerator that is on its back filled with green water, grit-slimy gravel on the bottom, and it smells a lot like sausage gravy. The fish/dog flaps thin tentacles that protrude from its belly, wiggling them throughout the thick liquid like they are keeping it afloat. It cannot bark anymore, but sometimes it will let out a growl, a bubbling of water and a deep rumble through the sides of the refrigerator. The gas station man is proud of his pet, admiring it with his twisting eyes and soggy grins. He brings my palm to its scaly back sometimes and rubs it along the globby hairs or some tentacles. I always cringe and pretend I am back home.

He tells me, "You know, Jesus Christ is staring at you from the bottom of the toilet water while you are sitting there, looking up at your feces as it creeps slowly out of you."

I just nod and try not to smell his seaweed/anchovy breaths, or look directly into his pointy eyes. He says he can see things very keenly with his eyes. He can even see the ghosts that wander our world between dimensions, even Jesus' ghost. He says Jesus has dark skin, bushy eyebrows, and a crooked nose. He says that he keeps to himself mostly, hardly ever seen walking with any of the other ghosts. "They don't seem interested in the messiah. Maybe they are disappointed that he is not as great as the bible says."

I wipe myself and pull my pants up really quick. I stare into the toilet to see if his reflection is shimmering in the water there. Nothing. Not even a crucifix. I flush it away, click-swirling down. If he had been there, his spirit would have been pulled through millions of plastic pipes across the landscape and into a monster septic tank that lives over the gloom-bitter mountain. He'd have to walk all day and most of the night to get back here. He probably wouldn't even bother.

I know I wouldn't bother. I've taken that hard blistering journey over the mountain, to the city of black machines that growl and sweat high into the cloud world, miles of motion, coughing churning, scream-steaming, a monster train that never departs. The walk is so long that your eyeballs puss over before you arrive, a greasy film that hazes you. Your pores bleed, your whole body shivers with weakness, and the thin windy air seems to sweep away strips of your skin.

Sometimes I'll go there to make sure the beasts are not broken down. Just making sure. I always shake my head once I get there, sit down, gasping, shaking my head. It's like checking to make sure the sky is still in the air. Such a long walk to prove myself an idiot. I usually contemplate putting my head into the teeth of one of those hungry beasts, allowing it to tear through my neck and unfold the skull into strings of red meat. But I never do it. The thought of meeting Jesus' ghost after my death continuously alters my suicide plans.

I step out of the bathroom, hoping Jesus isn't stalking behind me, to the droopy frizzle-crinky room which is the rest of my house. It squeezes around me, creeps its closeness into the pit of my brain.

I leave. Dart out of the door to the front porch, and it gives a sigh as I sit into it, ooze into the log made rocking chair. A splinter bites my thigh, but I allow it. The relaxation is pleasing, decent. A bottle of watermelon juice goes straight to my lips as I dream of a beautiful truck driver and her slender-curvy flesh parts.

My eyes go into the landscape:

Bland fields stretching miles in the black-grass valley. They are beneath a pink-speckled quivering sky, which seems to hang a little too close above me, like I am finely printed words that it is trying to read.

The fields grow a single year-round crop: hands.

Human beings have evolved to a point where hands are like the tails of lizards, just a little jerk in the right nerve and they pop off at the wrist. Just like that. But unlike the tails of lizards, human hands do not grow back. Evolution is strange how it goes sometimes. One day a man will make a living as a professional boxer, and the next his hands are falling off from doing too many pullups. It is quite irritating, even dangerous at times. But you can get new hands for a small amount of money. They sell them at supermarkets everywhere in the bigcity, right between the creamed socks and pickled candles, and the supermarkets get them from hand farmers like me.

The truck driver comes every other Thursday and picks up a load. She always smiles at me when she comes with BIG green-painted lips, twirling locks of her crazy-grass hair.

"They're always in demand," she says, but I hardly hear her. I am too busy picturing the two of us on a stroll in the fields, wrapped around each other without talk, or I think of awaking one night to find her in my bed, on top of me, channeling through my insides with her cherry eyeballs.

She doesn't talk to me about the bigcity, not even when I ask. I haven't seen it in years and wish she would take me there with her, see what has become of it, but she never tells me. I'm not sure it exists anymore.

Supposedly, there have been many changes. The man at the gas station says that beings from Saturn live among us now. He says they came in a ship resembling a dollar bill and now fill up ghettos along the west coast. I never talk to the gas station man. He tells me things, but I never tell him things. He is the only person for miles and I still don't tell him things. He tells me how the world has gone flat again, how people decided not to like Columbus anymore and so they cut the surface off the planet and flattened it out. It orbits the sun like a piece of paper these days, just beside the bald sphere. I am confused about which one we call Earth. When I dig, I am scared that I might go too far and create a BIG hole in the planet. I might even fall through and go tumbling forever.

I ask the truck driver if what the gas station man says is true and she smiles at me and blows bubbles with her raisin-flavored chewing gum. She is so exquisite with her looks, but she sometimes reminds me of an endless flight of stairs. That's what the gas station man calls me: an endless flight of stairs.

I wish the truck driver was here with me right now. She always cheers me up with her smile and eyeballs. She told me she would come early this week, but she has yet to show. I hope I have the courage to ask her to eat dinner with me this time. I have been planning out what I will say and have cleaned my house too. Well, mostly. Maybe I will just wait until next week.

I open a book. It is BIG and has lots of words in it. I take a chewed pen to it and draw a square around a paragraph. I color it in, ripping the paper slightly, and put flowers around the sides. I draw the sun with a scraggy beard and ears. I sometimes try putting the truck driver, but I can never her draw her as beautiful as she really is. Actually, I can't even draw her to look human. The gas station man says that the ghosts don't like my drawings. They think my art looks childish and he makes me so mad that I run away from him and throw rocks at plants.

However, I can draw parts of the truck driver. Her hair especially. I swirl lines on the page to and it looks just like her wild hair, and I can almost see her eyes underneath those hairs winking at me.

Then I notice a breath hitting the back of my neck.

I pause.

I don't turn around, joints stiff. Jesus Christ must be behind me. He's probably trying to look down my shirt to see my chest hairs.

I ignore him and continue with drawing. Cautiously, nerves twitching in my collar bone, I adjust my shirt flat to blind him from my torso skin. Immediately, I sense his disappointment in the air.

Looking to the distant mountain that blocks the machine world from visibility, I become inspired. I decide to draw it next to the truck driver's hair on the bundle of words, smiling and sipping watermelon juice as I go, thinking about drawing the machines on the next page.

"The machines run the world," the gas station man says.

He told me that they control the weather and the temperature of the planet. He also said that they control gravity and if the machines ever break down, we will float off the planet into space. The world would end if we didn't have them. Sometimes I get so worried about the machines breaking down that I can't sleep at night. I have to go check up on them. Take that long walk across the plane to see if they are okay.

I shriek as a breeze flushes through my pant leg, quickly slapping it shut. It must have been Jesus trying to feel up my leg. Jerk-standing, dropping my book to the dirt, I go into the fields to pace.

The man at the gas station says that sometimes Jesus is physically attracted to men, but is not actually gay. He will kiss you on the lips, but not in a sexual manner. Jesus is above sex. Or is Jesus sexually confused? I cover my mouth, just in case. I couldn't imagine having the savior's tongue slip into my lips when I am unaware.

I stomp my bare feet through rows of hands growing from the soil. The hands are almost fully ripe now. They are tight fists, raised in pride or maybe anger, thousands of them roaring, a crowd to a tyrant. Stampering the field, not turning around to my ugliness-home, knowing Jesus Christ is behind me.

The sky sinks lower, just a short distance from my head. It is trying to crush me, suffocate me. The man at the gas station says that the sky used to be a giant ocean, but the water got stretched out for miles-miles wide/high until it became a gas. He also says that someday it will compress back into an ocean and drown us all. I look up a lot these days.

I kick a growing fist off of its roots, then stomp it into the soil until I separate some fingers with my heel. My lungs break down to harsh whispers. I pause. My eyes go forward, imagining Jesus Christ masturbating with one of the hands in front of me, probably fantasizing my image as he does it. My throat goes sick, tendons stretching the neck skin.

I run away. Out of the field, down the road that knows the gas station and the highway. I don't go quickly, my bare feet slicing against the sharp gravel, blood trickling, a bruise under a toenail.

Rocks crash-scurry behind me, sounding as if coming to hit me. I think Jesus is throwing them, angered that I am leaving him. I don't turn around, moving faster despite the feet suffering. The noises continue, clinking rocks against one another behind me. I keep moving until the noise fades, Jesus giving up.

Ten minutes.

I find myself at the gas station and freeze.

Look back.

My house has disappeared from my sight, only a line of field can be seen from this distance. I turn to the gas station, then back to my house. Which is the lesser of two evils?

The perverted ghost of Christ or the man with the mutated dog? I choose the gas station man, hiking up to his tiny shack at the highway.

All along the sides of the road, I see white-painted animals frozen-posed at random. The gas station man enjoys capturing small animals and spray painting them until they go hard, then he places them around the outside of his house like lawn ornaments. They can be found all over the highway: rabbits, lizards, birds. It is his hobby. He is a very decorative man.

I approach him from behind as he empties gasoline onto the pavement and highway, his red flannel shirt flickering in the shatter-breeze. My sight goes to the street, down the wavy worm to the mountains, huge blues bulging from thunderclouds. The sky seems to be popping in places, sizzling, churkling, like it has a short circuit somewhere.

The gas station man hears me coming. "I haven't seen you in awhile," he says to me.

"I've been busy," I say, staring at the gas splashing on the street, but my voice was mumbled and he probably didn't hear me.

"Doing what? Watching the fists grow around you?"

I nod and look at the horizon that meets the road. It is purple and marble-swirly, whispering.

"Is Jesus behind me?" I ask, soft-trembling.

He turns to me with his needle eye-spins, clicking sounds, and looks over my shoulder, piercing into the other world. Then he goes back to his work.

"No," he answers. "There's no one behind you." He bites at a bumblebee circle-flying the gas stream. "Is Jesus bothering you?"

"The whole world is bothering me." My voice surprisingly loud.

"You know what I do when something is bothering me?" he asks.

I look at the dirt under my fingernails.

"That's right," he said. "I get rid of it."

A breeze scurry-swarms under my skin, nerves crawling, ticking.

"See," says the gas station man, "this highway's been giving me trouble lately. No one ever drives it anymore. I'm gettin' put out of business." He spits an oil-goo at my feet. "So I've decided to burn it down."

I nod at him, wandering my eyes across the terrain. I see a truck parked off the side of the road by the gas station. The truck driver's truck, muddy with a flat tire, black paint on the side with crude designs. But she is nowhere to be found.

"Where is she?" I ask the gas station man.

"Who?"

I clear my throat and speak louder, "The truck driver. Where is she?"

"Her truck broke down," the gas station man says with sincerity, shaking his head.

"Where is she?"

The gas station man's gas stream dies away, so he takes a hose from the next pump and continues.

"She's an interesting girl, isn't she?" he says.

I glance at the blood on my toes.

"Green hair, green lips, blood-red eyes." The gas station man licks his lips within wiry beard hair.

Pressure builds on my eyeballs, fists clenching.

"Blood red eyes," he says, smiling at me and nodding his head. "Bloody, blood red."

He laughs and sprays the gas like a sprinkler.

"What have you done with her?" I crack-scream at him.

The gas station man stares deep at me.

I say, "Where is she?"

Then he jumps, pointing over my shoulder and yelling, "Look, Jesus is behind you!"

I jerk around to see nothing, just open landscape and white animals.

"He's got his hand in your pants!" he screams at me.

"Quick, stop him!"

I throw my fists about, lunging away in squeals.

"He's under your shirt! Get him out of there!"

I run, fleeing the ghost. The gas station man is laughing at me as I go. His laugh scrapes the top of the mountain, screeching, driving blood to swell my brain.

Charging into his home, my feet too torn and raw to make it all the way to my own house. I slam the door shut and put my weight against it so that the Jesus ghost will not come inside.

The gas station man continues screeching his laughs from the highway. Through the window, I peek at him walking down the median, emptying a bucket of gas over his shoulders in the distance.

My standing grows tired so I slide down the crumbly door, turning to a tiny room without furniture. It is all white, rough white. A single blanket is on the wood floor in the corner, his bed, and there is a cage of rabbits, prairie dogs, turtles that are ready for spray painting. Under my black toes: wetness. I find a trickle-trail of blood there which leads across the room and disappears underneath a door.

I get to my sour feet—the gas station man's wild laugh persisting—step across the room to the door and open. Another blank white room. I didn't expect the gas station man's home to be so bland.

The blood is sprinkled to another room, also empty, and ends at a manhole in the center of the wood floor. I go to the rim and peer down. Inside of the hole: electric dark. Sparks twitching within. I descend to a crowd of television sets, no, computer screens, all around me. Their faces squeeze me in the shivering black, and as I look upon them, they show me familiar sights. I gasp, nearly fall to the ground.

Fists.

I see thousands of fists. *My* fists. Each computer screen shows a different angle of my field...and my porch, my house, *inside* my house.

I hold my breath inside of me, trying to calm. There have been little cameras hiding around my property this whole time, hiding within fists and within cracks of wood. Spying, keeping an eye on me.

From across the darkness, a splash of electricity lights the corner, sparks popping, blistering. Then a woman's cry bursting at me. It whines for a moment, then slides away.

I step closer, my eyes focusing into the dimness. A figure stands there, squirming, tied up maybe.

"What has he been doing to you?" I say.

It cries again, her voice gurgling, trying to form words.

When I step closer, I recognize a large sheet of glass separates us. A window.

"I'll get you out," I tell her, grabbing a computer and spinning it around to shine light on the glass, and she brightens.

The truck driver is naked in front of me, white skin swollen behind the glass, floating. She is in water, submerged within a tank of water. Her green hair waving in the thick liquid, green lips open to me. All of her is green now, tinted skin, turning scale-slimy. Tentacles are growing from her stomach and breasts, snaking through the fluid, just like the gas station man's dog. She is attached at the belly to a large cord, connected to a black machine beside her water tank.

A jolt of electricity hits her again, sparks flame-showering from the machine. She erupts from the water gargle-splashing, squawking at the pain, her naked body rubbing against the glass. Our eyes meet, her cherry-red eyes glowing into mine as she gasps for air, but nothing enters her lungs.

She fades down into the liquid, still gleaming into my eyes. Gills open up on her neck to breathe the water's air. Staring, just staring at me. Then she closes her eyes and feigns sleep. The tentacles flutter her until she turns around to expose a thin lump growing down her back, preparing to be a large ugly fin. My face contorts with disgust.

I explode from the house and into the red-smoky landscape. The highway is on fire. From horizon to horizon, the long highway has been set ablaze, demons dancing across the wind. I yell at it, rage at it, but it overpowers me, squeezes me into a ball.

I go to the gas station man's tool shed, fighting off the color red, screaming. I rip open the door and find a pickax under a wheelbarrow, then tear it out of the mess.

My hand falls off.

It pops off at the wrist as the pickax catches on a hose, and now it twitches spidery on the ground. I grab the fallen member with the surviving hand and toss it at the fire-highway, screaming redness, pounding my forehead into the metal shed.

I look for the gas station man, but I am alone. My second hand carefully pulls the pickax from the hose-knots and rests it on my shoulder, and I scan the landscape for him, screaming his name, craving to put him in a tank of electric water until he turns into a fish.

The demons within the wind open tar-mouths at me, moaning for escape as if prisoners within the smoke. My mind is chaotic, searching for the gas station man with sharp jerks of my vision.

There he is:

A bundle of blackness within the flames, burning like a tire. I run up to him, swinging the pickax inside the flames to get at him, but I cannot reach. The smoke burns my eyes closed and forces me back.

"Why?" I yell at the gas station man, tear-frustrated that I cannot hurt him. "Why, why, why?"

And my anger sends me charging away from the highway. I take the road back to my house, the flames following on my left, eating up the crop, running through the crowd of fists raised in my direction. As the fire reaches them, the fists open up to fry and melt. I lace boots onto my swollen feet and fit myself up for a new hand, a strong one that will hold.

The pickax in both of my fists and flames churkle-dancing the horizons, I turn away from the fields and the gas station, still screaming with rage but the screams have grown deeper like growls. And I start the long hike over the mountain. To the land of helpless black machines…to get rid of what's been bothering me.

Looking for a Name

Kevin L. Donihe

<*invocation*>

Let this transcript present my full character upon a sober reading. I proclaim this to be Truth on the 19th day of May in the Year of Our Lord (*Ackmed Nemrah Garnlarty*) 1998. This is the NAME OF POWER—enclose it with no quotation marks or periods. (Parenthesis, however, are okay.)

<*reality*>

Skeezer, Freezer, Weezer, Chuck, Canopy, Roger, Fox, Skank, Guinness…
Bear with me. I need to remember a name.

<*fantasy*>

I am the ungod of compassion, lost in a wellspring of discontent. Lost. Found. In a gutter filled with rain. Dropp'd off, floating at sea, tweedle-dee/tweedle-dee. I am ungod. Worship me like a motherfucker. Wrap me in the smooth, warm folds of your bosom. Take me in the mouth and do me on the lawn furniture of love. Do me in the plastic jacuzzi.

Wait…This is getting pornographic. I think I'm losing sight of my true aggression. But I'm coming back now. I feel it. A sense of self burns inside. It seems to have mass. Mass can never be created or destroyed. I AM BACK. I have returned from the brink. I (he) am the observer, the scientist. He studies me and I hear his (my) voice. He is the archetype of my true self that keeps my (our) body running. He talks like Humphrey Bogart. I am now relating Truth to you. Future generations, heed my gospel of love. I am now the Ungod Zorax—founder of light and hedonism. I am the gospeler of the psalms lost to the Ages on his way to Calcutta. I am the delivery-man who walks along the alleyways, muttering to himself because his wife won't give him any in the back of his 1956 Plymouth Firebird. She is a bitch—a heartless, mindless, arrogant whore. I now know how to retrace subjects again. Writing this sentence, however, I lost it…

<reality>

Skeezer, Freezer, Weezer, Chuck, Canopy, Roger, Fox, Skank, Guinness...
Ah, fuck it!

Anyway, I've long had delusions of grandeur—the greatest intellect, the greatest lover, etc, etc, etc, oh well. It's true. I think I'm God. I really do. I think I can never die yet I fear death around every corner. Irrational measures make up my rational mind. I am the everyday product of fear.

My entire life has been a script—pre-planned, pre-thought.

<fantasy/reality>

Tell me the Truths of Amon-Re. I am the ungod who wants you to stay at home tonight under the protective canopy of your soul. Do me in the arms of Morpheus. I am the ungod of Purgatory. Find me in the red mark shopping list found at the five-and-dime on April 20, 1956. This is the way of SHUNTA—non-goddess of the non-world and surveyor of all she sees. She is the many-starletted whore who takes men into her mouth and delivers them into a world of pleasure and death. Fuck, this is becoming clichéd.

Wait...I seem to be finding myself again. Lost in the folds of delusion as I so often am. I can breathe now. I feel free from this computer-tether. OH MY GOD, I SEE THE LIGHT...of faith. FUCK! I'm only imitating Skeezer, Freezer, Weezer, Chuck, Canopy, Roger, Fox, Skank, Guinness—what was his fuckin' name! (It was really weird.) He had this image engraved on his wallet. A stick figure holding its arms to Heaven. He carved this and then he smiled a lot. No more troubles. No more worries. I couldn't figure out how he pulled it off but maybe I can. Someday. Maybe if I remember his name. I am ungod. Feel me roar in the righteous slumber that coils you back into earthen arms.

Damn it, I LOST MYSELF AGAIN!

<reality>

FUCK YOU!!! Why the hell don't you love me? Why am I the one thrown out of houses? Why am I the one always referred to as "that guy on the couch"? I truly hate this. Does my voice sound bad? Do I look gay? Is my ego too strong and do I need to curb it? Stop feeding the id?

Do I try too hard? What do you see when you look at me through the mirror in your eyes? I often imagine myself in movies. In them I have to talk and act perfect. That might explain a lot of things. I need to be the control-freak, the grand high priest generalissimo.

And what about meaning? Do you think it exists? Or is everything just a by-product of psychosomatic engineering? I have memories. (At least I think I do. Some of them seem older than me.) It doesn't matter though. They're trapped. They can't find their way out of my head. I don't want them to find their way out. They've been in there longer than me. They know what I don't know. And they flaunt it.

<fantasy>

I know everythink. I am the Judge-Penitent. Ungod of those whose mental capacities won't let them see "the real you". ("You" being "I" in this case.)

Just the other day I thought the thought I had thought about thinking when I considered the cabbages, sprung from their cages and lost to the growing Oriental hordes that invade my subconscious much like a Boeing 747 readying for takeoff. Terminal velocity—the speed at which the doughnut ceases flying and starts to hover above the dining room floor. Non-propulsion liftoff. Break the sound barrier. Land on the moon.

Fuckin' silly, ain't it?

<existential screaming angst>

BUT I WILL LIVE TO PROVE ALL THE BASTARDS AND ASSHOLES WRONG! DAMN THEM TO HELL AND TO THE LIVING NIGHTMARE THEY DRAGGED ME INTO! DAMN THE ONES WHO MADE ME PERFORM FOR THEIR AMUSE-MENT! DAMN THE ONES WHO HELD MY TINY SHIRT TO THEIR CHESTS IN THE MEN'S LOCKER ROOM! DAMN THE ONES WHO USED ME AS A BAR TO BENCHPRESS! DAMN THE ONES WHO CALLED ME GAY! DAMN THE ONES WHO THOUGHT I DIDN'T KNOW WHAT A PIECE OF MY OWN ANATOMY WAS, AND DAMN ME FOR PERPETRATING ALL THIS UPON MYSELF!

AND WHERE IS GOD? WHERE IS GOD WHEN I NEED HIM? DESERTER OF MAN! FOUL, UNNATURAL THING THAT WIELDS ITS POWER WITH THE WILL OF A THOUSAND MEN, CLUSTERED IN THE HALLWAYS OF DEATH!

<reality>

I looked up and felt suddenly different. Perhaps the old me is finally coming back. Alcohol can only last so long. Now what was that guy's name?

Remembering it will be a simple thing, but it'll make all the difference in the world.

<outside/inside observer>

I am the scientist writing all this stuff down. The "we." The many locked up inside the one.

The old boy is coming back. *Finally.* He will not understand this later. He *never* understands what I have to say. I think he has to figure it all out for himself. Taking this message from the Other World will help. He unconsciously tried before, but he couldn't read his own writing. He needs a friend, someone to translate. I am that friend. That friend he needs more than life itself. I am the scientist, the observer caught up in suspenders of light that run beneath the foundations of faith.

<reality>

I hope nobody reads this or ever finds it. But this is the truth about me, and I must reveal it as soon as possible. I must carry this text on my person at all times. I have to be reminded or else I'll forget. But it's not the key. No. I know what the key is but I can't get it out of my head. Is it time for another cigarette? Not quite, I must think of that name first. Then I'll be released. Skeezer, Freezer, Weezer, Chuck, Canopy, Roger, Fox, Skank, Guinness. (I've said these before.) It's a weird name. He's got a weird wallet and smiles a weird smile. He knows something that I do not know. (Faith.) He's felt something I have not felt. (Happiness.) He's got a weird name. A weird name. That's all I know.

Wait…

Tinker.

<outside/inside observer>

Well. It seems I'm not needed here anymore.

(scientist departs)

(dies)

Ecphoriae

Forrest Aguirre

I look at my hands, sporadic bursts of light from flashlights down the drainage tunnel splay across the weight in my palms, burning a white image into my eyes—a ceramic skull, sans mandible, somewhere between homo erectus and homo sapiens sapiens. Ten round buttons are embedded in the bregma, in a circle, like a crown. Each button, concave for the push of fingers—fingers much smaller than my own—is carved with a stylized sigil reminiscent of those symbols found in the colonial-era archaeological digs at Mohenjo-daro and Harrapa, abstracted images of flax, bulls, water jugs: the tools and goods of everyday domestic farming.

I believe that each of the buttons corresponds to our numbers one through ten. At least I use this code to make sense of the symbols, making a mental note of the combinations I have tried, along with the result of each series. Five-digit series activate the skull. I have no way of knowing whether the buttons correspond to our numbers or any other abstraction, for that matter. The language of the crown is beyond dead. It is cast into oblivion, as I soon may be. If the men coming down the sewage tunnel take the skull from me—and they surely will: they are brutes, animals in neat black suits (I have no strength left to fight them)—oblivion might be humanity's shared lot.

I punch in a combination.

1-1-1-3-4

An indigo light glows in the left eye socket, midnight cerulean orbital fissure brightening to ice blue. Static projections flicker out from the hole in a virtual photon aerosol, then coalesce into the foot high image of a woman in a flowing night gown, Victorian, by the frilly lace.

She tugged at her long black tresses with both hands and screamed soundlessly like crazed Ophelia.

She dissipates into the air, her molten luminescence fading to black as she backed away from some unseen dread.

This vision cannot help me now.

Only briefly, by the light of the holograph, do I see. Coal-ash darkened cement walls like a dripping castle dungeon. Bits of trash. A rusted can. Crumpled papers. My dessicated leather shoes, laces shredded. Threadbare trousers, brown, I think. Rat's eyes.

Is smells of piss and mold. The salt of sweat trickles past my lips, puckers the tongue. I am cold and shaking, rough concrete scraping my back as I shiver. Voices shout down the concrete corridor. I am their destination. I am running out of combinations.

5-7-1-1-3

SKRTCH "Databank empty. Please make another selection."

Validity is a matter of collective acceptance. The idea of "history," for example, with its assumption of past, present, and future chronological structures, is accepted by many as a valid worldview. But it is, after all, only one way of looking at the world, of containing our conceptions, of keeping us sane. It is, at its best, unimaginative. At its worst, it is inevitable. That is, if you accept it as valid at all. I have learned to reject chronology and history. Uncertainty, chaos, these are the underlying structure of the universe, and of my narrative, should I ever be allowed to finish it. To be frank, I mistrust my own memories, which have become so bound up in the skull's vignettes (more of them later) that it is difficult to differentiate the two. I am the proverbial unreliable narrator.

Unreliability seems to me a trait I have developed over the course of years, almost a skill. Melinda would remind me frequently that she could not count on me for anything.

"But I'm providing for the two of us."

"A post-doctoral stipend is hardly providing. I work full-time too, remember? And my students don't really want to be in class, they're forced to by law. Besides, the extra hours you're spending doing research," (I cannot accurately describe the disdain with which she said the word) "make your stipend even less meaningful."

"Well, at least I don't eat dinner. The coffee I get at night is cheaper than a meal!" I tried to inject some humor into the confrontation.

"Not funny."

I failed.

And Melinda was not finished, though she paused for a few deceiving seconds, gathering her strength before pressing again.

"Ryan, what do you do all night at your lab? Are you even at your lab?"

"You know I am. You've called me there."

I thought I had disarmed her with my sidelong accusation of spying.

I was wrong.

"Who else is there with you?"

I stood silent, heart racing. It was as if my brain and my mouth wouldn't agree. I was not a good liar, but revealing the truth would have more serious consequences, I felt, than to falsely admit an affair, if that was what she suspected.

As the internal debate raged within me, Melinda broke the silence.

"I've heard voices in the background, Ryan. And they aren't the radio. Someone else has been there at night with you, Ryan."

"Co-workers," I lied.

"Co-workers," she repeated flatly.

I told you I was not a good liar, as unreliable as I may be.

What was I supposed to tell her? "Honey, I'm studying recordings stored in a mechanical skull that I suspect is tens of thousands of years old that I dug up while doing research in eastern Congo"? I might as well have lied and told her that I was having an affair with a hard-bodied sophomore named Jenna, but I didn't want to hurt Melinda. The romance may have seeped out of our marriage, but I still loved her and didn't want to see her hurt. Besides, I've already told you several times, I'm not a good liar.

Not that I had a chance to make up such a lie. She left immediately.

4-6-5-3-2

The view is unchanging for days. Rain falling in large droplets, pooled onto large jungle canopy leaves, then knocked down by chimpanzees or silverbacks as they pass through the trees above. There is light, of a sort, but it bleaches everything within sight to a pale green-grey. Then night falls and all is black except for the occasional pair of feline eyes that swallow up all available light, then give it back through a pair of golden disks. Again, the sun rises somewhere far beyond the chlorophyll mesh. A river of fire ants rushes by, flooding toward a wounded okapi. The animal's bones soon glisten red with the swarm, then bleed to chalk as the ants move on, hunting for their next meal. Night falls, dawn rises, the cycle repeats again and again, the field of vision obscured from time-to-time by some titanic animal—larger than an elephant—that lumbers through the jungle, a shape rarely seen, even in late Lemurian times, in the years following The Awakening. After a long, long time (as measured by man), a white hand (how long—as measured by man—has it been since I last saw a white hand?) reaches down, lifts (the field of vision widens), turns to face the observer to the observed (a plain looking man of middle age, not athletic, like the bodies of those I have occasionally seen shooting projectiles at one another, slaying others with machetes), then complete and utter blackness.

I had found it while collecting forensic evidence of retaliatory killings of Hutu by Tutsi in the refugee camps in the Kigali region, years after the 1994 genocide. The moment I spotted it lying in some muck on the jungle floor, I knew it was a rare find. Perhaps I should have left it so that we (there were others on the expedition, though I was quite alone when I stumbled upon the skull) could have established provenience. But something compelled me to take the skull and stuff it in a bag before anyone else noticed. My ego was surely the bait, but something external—a rush of adrenaline? The desire to keep a dark secret in that place where I was tasked with bringing the hidden to light?—set the hook in me, and I bit down hard.

It took several days before I could examine it alone. One night, beneath a mosquito net, by the light of a sputtering propane lantern, I withdrew the macabre trophy from my backpack. I had planned to give it an old-fashioned phrenological exam. I thought it clever of me to do so in the very area of the world where phrenology, under the auspice of Belgian and German colonial rulers, had entrenched the previously-unheard-of notion that "Hutu" and "Tutsi" were physiologically different classes of human beings. I would examine a modern faux-skull using the same techniques that began the chain of events that would lead the skull to be there in the first place.

But the skull did not want to cooperate.

Or, rather, it cooperated all too well.

3-3-1-4-7

A storm was raging outside, blue waves crashing into the iron pylons a thousand feet below the crescent-shaped building in which the group sat. A trio of scientists, albinos all, sat across a large semi-circular table set exactly contrary to the building's orientation. Everything was in contrast—the geometrics of furnishings with room furnished, white skin and somber pink eyes on extravagant black outfits, even the sound of the tempest-strewn sleet that slapped against the curved windows was a foil to the mellifluent voice of the man who stood behind the table.

"Our civilization is dying," he said without emotion.

The woman sitting to his left blinked back a tear.

The woman sitting to his right stared straight ahead, glaring with malice.

"Even the climate is set against us. The ice is expanding on one side, even as the Atlantean forces advance on the other. Lemuria cannot, will not, survive. Given the thoroughness of our enemy's conquest, it is unlikely, even, that myths will be left behind after they are done."

He took his seat, turning to the woman on his left. His long nose, in profile, gave him the appearance of a bird, a pale raven, gaunt and brooding.

The woman stood, straightening her back as if to slough off the emotion she had earlier displayed.

"You are aware of yourself. We have tested you, and our tests have proven successful. We have created, in you, the most versatile and resilient recording device in the history of the world. You will carry within you a record of this people. Though Lemuria's utter destruction is inevitable, you will preserve our memory."

The second woman, by far the tallest of the three, spoke:

"We estimate that you will have several years in which to collect data and document our civilization. We have implanted in you a few very basic recordings which should allow you to contextualize your observations and have programmed in you those instinctive reactions that will help you to avoid harm. We have built you to last for eons, moving freely among the Atlanteans and their descendants, disguised as one of their kind. Your memory shall be, is, perfect. We have intentionally voided any potential for emotion in your makeup. You are self-aware, but objectively so. As you go about our cities, observing and recording, noting our achievements in art, beauty, knowledge, prowess, poetry, and philosophy, you will become, are, our repository of truth."

She sat down heavily in her chair, exhausted, then unceremoniously slumped down. Her companions looked at her, their faces twisting in fear as they realized that her collapse was accompanied by a sudden inrush of air from a pebble-sized hole that had appeared in the windows to her side. Air and water sprayed in from that hole as the pressure differential between the atmosphere outside and that of the room rushed toward equilibrium. Before it was attained, however, another hole appeared, then another, and another. The others fell on the first, neat red holes showing in their albino skin.

A fine mist now filled the room, and the sky immediately outside the erstwhile windows—they had shattered to tiny shards of puzzled glass—darkened with large mechanical shapes that blocked out what little light the storm clouds had let through. The roar of the machines engines' harmoniously melded with the crash of waves, the whine of the wind that now so fiercely coursed through the ruined windows.

Contradiction was blown away as a dozen Atlantean commandoes, fully three heads shorter than the dead albinos, even with the distinctive Atlantean combat armor exoskeleton, came through what remained of the windows. They approached, removing their goggled helmets, smiling at their black compatriot, extending their gauntleted hands in greeting.

"Brother! We are here to rescue you!"

I was careful to keep the artifact concealed. As I look at it, I wonder how it could have come through undetected, even with the laxity of customs agents, who assumed that we, as anthropologists and academics, would never stoop so low as to illegally import artifacts or trophies. We were, after all, not treasure hunters.

It is only after a few moments that I recall that the number-pad atop the skull's head was covered by a scalp of burnt skin—or some material approximating skin—when I first discovered it. Scraps of "skin" still fleck the parietals, but the charred monk's pate is now gone, has been gone since I examined the thing late at night in my campus office after successfully smuggling it through in a box of bones that I legitimately needed for my research.

The excitement I felt while sneaking my morbid prize through customs intensified, through some perversion of intellectual curiosity, the interest in the object. My research soon veered away from the concerns for which I was hired and toward the skull. Artificial class struggles, the encoding of colonial prejudices in a post-colonial society, even the genocide itself, could wait. It is still waiting.

7-1-9-5-2

Lawokadia, Nantende, and Kubundu elicit roaring laughter the moment they step out on stage. Their faces are painted white, then blackface over the false white. Two of them wear Belgian army uniforms, one wears a tuxedo; all three wear a black top-hat with the lid cut off. A brilliant bouquet of flowers thrusts out of the top of each as if the hats were tall black vases. The immediacy of the drama draws the crowd in, the triple-layered makeup and fantasy of black mocking white mocking black enmeshes them. The audience's attention is centered on the trio. Observations can be made from very near the audience, immediately adjacent to them, in fact, barely obfuscated by a thin veil of elephant grass and overhanging palm leaves.

They stand, backs straight, heads slightly tilted back to allow a faux-haughty look at the audience members. The trio smile and widen their eyes in unison, as if they are controlled by some unseen puppet master. Their expressions are exaggerated, eyes large, as if with surprise, smiles spread to the point of exposing almost every one of their teeth. There are 82 teeth between the three of them. Kubundu is missing the most.

They speak with feigned European feigning African accents.

Nantende: "Mine brothers, we are here on this spesheeyal occasion…"

Lawokadia: "Ja, this occasion."

Kubundu (whose lack of teeth makes him sound, ironically, as if teeth are rattling around in some unseen cavity in his head. He does not understand the irony.): "What occasion, mine brother?"

Nantende: "The funeral of owa good leada, Mobutu Sese Seko."

Lawokadia (with surprise): "He dead? Mobutu Sese Seko, the old leopard, dead?"

Kubundu: "Who dat?"

The crowd bursts into laughter.

Lawokadia and Nantende look confused.

The crowd laughs on, even harder.

Kubundu (looking serious, which sends the audience into paroxysms of laughter): "Who is that?"

The observed is now viewing the observer.

Kubundu points, Nantende and Lawokadia take their hats off and peer.

The wind blows, the veil wavers and, eventually, the crowd turns to see what it is that the actors are staring at.

The actors' eyes widen, this time with worry.

The wind blows again.

Laughter dies.

The crowd takes up machetes, clubs, whatever is at hand. The observer turns, runs, trips, is overtaken. Feet surround the observer. The whistle of a downward-hacking machete fills the aural sensors. There is a loud "chunk"! The body is slashed into ribbons, the head accidentally kicked into the jungle during the slaughter.

My narrative will, undoubtedly, raise questions of tense. Perhaps it already has. Or, if this paragraph spurs your thoughts, it does so now.

But, you see, tense only matters insofar as it informs the narrative itself. Matters to the reader, that is. For instance, the present tense is, in Western culture, the most seemingly formal of the three tenses. It is clinical, academic, even unfeeling. Ironically, by trying to include the reader in "the moment," through the use of present tense, the writer actually interjects a sense of temporal and spatial distancing between the reader and the story. This exposition in the present tense is a case in point. Past tense, being the most familiar tense (on the written page, though not necessarily in conversation), is the most opaque and, possibly, the most versatile of the tenses. The future tense, with its prophetic stylings, is unwieldy and bombastic. Its irony is that while it portends future events, its structure seems archaic.

Note that I have not (ah, that comfortable past tense!) addressed the issue of chronology here. Nor will I ("And it will come to pass…") address it at length, only to point out that I reserve the right (note how the academic use of the present tense gives the sense of a contractual agreement) to use whatever tense I see fit to contextualize the narrative, which will (and has) color(ed) the reader's emotional response (or lack thereof) to the text itself. I refuse to become a slave to chronology. I have bent it for my own purposes, I am bending it for my own purposes, and I shall bend it for my own purposes (rather than "I will bend it for my own purposes," which, in the strictest sense, is a statement of desire rather than a statement of future action).

Chronology be damned. I am about to die.

I found myself spending long hours at night in my office pressing button combinations and watching the subsequent recordings, usually a holographic projection of a scene, sometimes bordered by strange floating symbols that I gather must have been some kind of data measurements or analytical tools measuring events in some way unknowable to me. Days bled together and I would sometimes find myself sleeping at my desk, the skull staring at the top of my own skull, my drool collecting on the veneer. I ate exclusively from a snack machine down the hall, and when I had the misfortune of seeing a colleague, would be told that I should go home and get some rest.

Eventually I did.

Melinda was not there.

Nor were most of her things.

Some did stay behind, however. As I walked down the hall from the living room to our bedroom—my bedroom, now—I took an ambulating inventory of the wall to my right, half a gauntlet of memory:

A calendar with images from the Hubble telescope, my wife's one concession of wall space outside of my den. It had not been flipped from the previous month. Each square day was full of strangers' names and times in Melinda's florid handwriting, an inscrutable manuscript, as alien to me in both content and time as the Cone Nebula that surmounted the writings.

The bathroom doorway, innocuous, except for a sliver of missing white paint, which reveals beneath it a shocking lozenge of pink. The original owners had built the room as a nursery, though their only pregnancy ended in miscarriage. When Melinda and I discovered we could not have children, I converted it into a bathroom. The irony of the change still strikes me as both funny and sad.

A painting, in dull brown and false greens, of a mountain range as seen from the area where my wife had been raised. I found the painting—and the area it portrayed—lifeless and boring. The mountains were an appropriate symbol of the barrier between us that had been forming even before my trip to Africa. Melinda preferred the windward side, I the leeward, she, life—or the life that would never be, that of a child we could never have, I, death—or the symbol of death inherent in the skull.

Another door, the hallway closet door. Behind it the plastic flotsam of a motherhood that never was and never would be. In the darkness, empty bins await diaper wipes and crayons, unused binders yawn their mouths wide after non-existent birth certificates, finger paintings, and report cards.

A pentangle of five picture frames, each holding two pictures: One of me on the left, one of Melinda on the right, a photographic procession through time, a mnemostic labyrinth, counter-clockwise. Ryan—I use the third person because I cannot recall a memory of the time at which the picture was taken—and Melinda as infants (in black and white), toddlers (in flat, muted color tones), adolescents (in sharper color, which accentuated their out-of-fashion clothing), teens (the memories return—I had forgotten to wear a dress shirt for picture day, so I wore a concert jersey over a white collared shirt borrowed from the photographer. Melinda was immaculate. Our hair was the same length, at the time), as newlyweds (still in separate photos from the same day). In the center of the spiral, a photo of one of our anniversaries. Fifth? Seventh? Tenth? Difficult to tell, without a child to mark time. I stopped taxing my brain with the effort of remembering, though the light brown hair in the photo had since gone grey, so it must have been quite a while ago. Not that it mattered now, back then.

With a great deal of difficulty, I turned away from the pictures and entered my den. I withdrew the skull, which I had carried under my trenchcoat, just in case Melinda was there when I came home. I decided then that I probably wouldn't need to worry about that again

2-2-1-5-5

"Dr. Klaar, this one claims his name is Mbutu," a civil service bureaucrat, ebony skin against pure white medical gowns, tapped a stethoscope against his thigh as he waited in the doorway for a response from the doctor.

"One moment," Dr. Helmuth Klaar, short and pudgy, dressed inappropriately for the African clime in a herringbone suit and bow tie, adjusted an immense set of calipers before walking over to the examination chair. "Send him in." Flies buzzed out into the waiting room upon the assistant's exit.

The civil servant ushered a short, ochre-skinned man into the doctor's office. "*Tunaenda Offisini kwa Doctori*," the taller man ordered the pygmy.

"Have him sit on the examination table, then leave us, the doctor instructed.

"Yes, sir," the servant saluted as if he were still an *askari*—he had been, in fact, in the days of the early European expeditions, if his decorations were any indicator. He wheeled about and exited the room, the tinkling of his medals fading into the distance.

Doctor Klaar approached the pygmy, placing the spanners across the man's head, taking rapid measurements from several angles with a deft precision. "Mbutu, eh? That doesn't sound like a local name."

"*Hapana*, Doctor, no."

"You speak Swahili and German well enough."

"I have traveled," a contemplative pause, "much, Herr Doktor."

"Well, don't travel off that chair, my vagabond friend. I'll need you to sit quite still while I take some measurements."

The doctor twisted open the calipers, sizing the pygmy's head: metopic suture to foramen magnum, left to right superciliary arches, right to left temporal lines, wormian bone to frontal squama. He checked the patient's eyes, nose, ears, then felt the lymph nodes. He set the calipers down, then made careful notes, hurriedly scribbling calculations in the margins, on a clipboard. The doctor's expression turned from jaded boredom to brow-wrinkling intrigue as he examined the subject's head with bare hands.

"Mbutu, have you been injured recently?"

"*Hapana.*"

"But your sutures…were you born with this?"

"Not born, Herr Doktor."

Profound amazement swept over Doctor Klaar's face as he smoothed the skin over the top of the man's skull, then kneaded it into small mounds, like a barber giving a scalp massage. He shuddered briefly as the skin gave way in one spot, tearing under his fingers, then the doctor steadied himself against the back of the examination chair, faint. He took a towel from a nearby drawer and, placing it on the patient's head, said, in a whisper, "We will speak of this to no one!"

The preceding paragraphs are, at worst, a lie, at best, a falsely-recalled memory. The incident took place—that I can confirm with the press of a few buttons. The words are correct, more or less: my German is rusty and my Swahili is anything but fluent, but I've caught the meaning of the words, if not their nuances.

The issue is not with the event, it is a question of the recollection of the event and its telling. The event is recorded in the skull's databank and can be replayed *ad infinitum*, if need be. But my narration of the event cannot be true because I see Mbutu—the skull (he, or it, has gone by many names, I have learned)—from outside the skull, whereas the data was collected through the "eyes" and "ears" of the skull. I have portrayed my thoughts on what the incident would have looked like had I been there. Such a telling of the story absolutely must involve a subconsciously-subjective interpretation of the situation. I may have portrayed the doctor in a more comical light than the skull observed, for instance. The face of Mbutu is fiction informed by a few glances of distorted reflections in mirrors or water, and is likely a melding of those reflections with the images of the Atlanteans among whom he traveled, before their untimely demise, and after whom the Lemurians had modeled his appearance. It is a montage, not a reproduction.

Lately, all of my thoughts have seemed like that—partially my own, partially those of an outside observer. My consciousness is shattering. Or, perhaps, it is coalescing.

My life could fly apart at any moment, if I was not careful. I reasoned, however, that my profession and my obsession could peacefully co-exist if I could somehow provide justification for the skull's existence. A few papers on skull worship and totemic construction in Central Africa would set the stage for the eventual revelation of the skull's existence. But a stage without a finale is empty of entertainment. I needed to know the end from the beginning, so I set about searching for the target.

There were hints and inferences, tiny cultural shards that reflected truth across the chronological wastelands of hidden eons. The Jericho skulls, circa 7000 B.C., plaster covered skulls with shells that represented eyes, stored beneath dwelling-place floors, probably for the purposes of ancestor worship. Another instance of shells-as-eyes came from the famous idol of Tezcatlipoca, and Aztec creator god, god of sorcerers, and so forth. The shells, however, provided only a lining, like mascara, to the iron pyrite pupil-less orbs. Besides, the loose association between shells and an Atlantis that was underwater only after this skull's creation was too tenuous. And the artifact that I held was Lemurian, not Atlantean. I needed evidence of that forgotten albino kingdom, but Atlantis' wholesale extinction of their ancient enemy would make such evidence sparse, indeed. Anything but a direct link would land my writings in the new-age section of the bookstore, alongside the hippies-channeling-extraterrestrial-spirits-with-crystal-dolphins-emitting-rainbows-on-their-cover-books. I would simultaneously die of starvation and embarrassment.

The jade-encrusted skull at the Monte Alban Tomb 7 in Oaxaca, Mexico was no help, either. And the Sedlec Ossuary was so far removed, chronologically and geographically, from anything that could be termed prehistoric Lemuria (and the skull was prehistoric, that I can assure you, though a future find—likely in Antarctica—will surely explode our ideas of history) that forging a link there was such a long shot as to be entirely not worth the effort.

I needed answers, and I needed them faster than I was finding them, else I ended up either destitute or among the ranks of Von Daniken, Labour and Gray, or Bill Kaysly. My only other option was to abandon the skull, and that I would not do.

The paucity of historical threads was disturbing, and I determined that I must approach the issue obliquely. If I could not make a direct connection, then I must use the skull's visions to trace back to events heretofore unknown to the historians, the anthropologists, even the earth scientists and astronomers. I would, over time, weave them into my net and draw them to the inevitability of the skull and its creators, direct historical link or not.

You will understand the predicament. Had I produced (or found, I am an honest man) some obscure reference that pointed directly to the existence of the skull and its purpose, would you then have been willing to suspend your disbelief? Or are you so unimaginative that without the faux reality of moving picture and sound, you could not bring yourself to believe such a fantastical yarn? Perhaps you want a plot filled with excitement and great acts of heroism, an adrenaline rush tale full of svelt gymnasts-cum-investigators and sweltering sexpots?

Well, I am no such person, and I strongly suspect that you aren't either. I am a professor of anthropology, not a writer. I am of average appearance, slightly overweight, mildly asthmatic, and, up until I found the skull, led an uninteresting domestic life. I am your narrator, love me or leave me. This is my plot, disordered, chaotic, and as true as the hands and feet of those who, in a few moments, will end any designs I ever had of revealing their creation, or, more properly, those of their ancestors.

I have reason to be a bit testy.

Back to the narrative, I haven't much time.

I began finding the binding points, tying the knots of the net. I uncovered Gimbutas' Earth Mother in a Romanian omphalic grave from five thousand years before the esteemed professor's statuary, thrusting the veil back further toward the original Earth Mother (a rather fat Lemurian as ugly as the statues—I won't pretend to understand the "prehistorics'" notion of beauty, but suffice it to say that she was a celebrity before the Atlanteans tore down her pinups and slew her stud-attendants). I justified Santillana and Von Deckend, to some degree, though they could not have known that the ancients' knowledge of the Precession of the Equinoxes so predated Hipparchus as to make him a mere scientific infant, in hindsight. They were correct in their supposition that the sorcerers and magicians merely preserved the truth, though these seers knew not from whence it came. I alone knew where the true knowledge of the heavens had originated.

Or so I thought.

There were, I would find, more who knew.

Recall Doktor Klaar. Recall Lawokadia, Nantende, and Kubundu. Read back, if you must. There is no shame in faulty memory, it is quite natural to us, especially if you are the middle-aged reader I suspect you are.

As a part of my studies, I set about to reconstruct the events between Doktor Klaar's discovery and Mbutu's decapitation.

3-5-7-1-0

She flipped her hair back in unabashed flirtation, wanton.

"I want you, little man," she cooed. Her French-accented German signified either Swiss extraction or an upbringing in Alsace-Lorraine sometime after the Franco-Prussian War. It was difficult to determine her age. Smoking and a lack of sleep might have explained the crows' feet around her eyes. Her libido was, in any case, intact. She reached out and stroked the observer's head with one hand while struggling away the strap of her dress with another. In the throes of her passion, she pressed hard on the observer's scalp, pulling the head toward her by force, stopping short of kissing it by a projection that had suddenly appeared in the air in front of her.

Had the ice not been stained red, the pile of limbs, trunks, and heads might have been mistaken for a drift of snow in a blizzard, a miles-long drift coated in large flakes. The blizzard might also have been mistaken for real snow, had the vision not panned to the side to reveal scores of Atlantean soldiers wielding flamethrowers among the remnants of what was once several thousand Lemurians, stripped of clothes and left to run in vain, for the sport of the conquerors. The air was thick with ash.

She backed away from the genocidal revelation, knocking over a kerosene lantern that quickly splashed its contents at the base of the bedroom door. By the time she had taken two steps back, the doorway was engulfed. She looked at the observer with a pleading fear in her eyes.

Doktor Klaar would not approve.

I learned the whereabouts of the conflagrated estate by triangulating between the skull's visions, inferences arising from my limited knowledge of African history, and through weeks worth of reading from Die Kolonial Zeitung on a microfiche reader in the university library's basement. My digs and discoveries had allowed me the luxury of applying for travel grants that included stipends that could make a man of modest means in the industrialized world a prince in the third. I set off for Namibia to study ancestral lore among the autochthons of the region, many of whom served as drillers in the diamond mines of Southern Africa—oh, how the Atlanteans had fallen—but took a week to swing by Doktor Klaar's dilapidated estate mansion in the mountains of central Tanzania, now owned by a cacao farmer who had prospered, of late, through the careful marketing of antioxidants in the United States.

It was there in a tour group composed exclusively of foreigners that I knew I was being followed.

My stalker, a tall, slender man of Swedish or Norwegian stock, made little attempt to disguise his intention to follow me wherever I went. I first noticed him back in the Namibian diamond mines, acting as some sort of consulting engineer, I presume, given the fact that he was never without a rolled-up blueprint under his arm. He would stare at me while I performed my interviews, never attempting to avoid my return stares. He would snort out his disdain then slowly walk off, turning again and again to look at me, sizing me up; preparing for a challenge. He would disappear for days at a time, only to return and begin his obnoxious behavior again.

At the plantation, I took a moment to go to the public restroom (it used to be a cattle-feeding trough before the walls were added) to relieve myself. I opened the door to find the man who had, unbeknownst to me, entered my tour group somewhere near Iringa. He was at a mirror, putting in a colored contact, blue to disguise the true pink of the eye I saw exposed in the mirror. He hesitated, finger poised in front of his face, smiled when he saw me in the reflection, then slowly put the contact in, staring at my reflection the entire time. I was close enough to notice, now, that his blond hair had been dyed. The underlying roots were white.

He left. I stood at the stall, but was too frightened to relax. I held it in until the tour bus arrived at the hotel, two hours later. My stalker never entered the hotel. I still worry whenever I enter a public restroom.

And now I sit in a sewage tunnel, unsure, at this point, which memories are mine and which are the skull's. I wish I could say I was drunk—I feel drunk, at least the ill effects of being drunk—but I am quite sober. Here is what I see, for my thoughts and the foregoing narration tick time differently, the telling of the tale has been the blink of an eye for me, but several thousand words for you.

I see a pair of rat's eyes turn, then I see the silhouette of the rodent as revealed to me by the reflection of flashlights off a puddle of brown liquid. I note, as the lights become more constant, that my pants only appear brown because of the muck smeared over the torn grey nylon. My shoes are in ribbons, and only the biting cold numbs me to the pain of my bleeding feet. A wad of papers rolls as the approaching figures invite a rush of even colder air down the tunnel. I had earlier tried to destroy those papers, but my pursuers were too swift. No matter, it is too late for concealing evidence now. They will have it all in a moment. There are six of them, including my "friend" from Africa. They have cast away their contacts and washed out their hair dye and, in the light of the flashlights that they are setting upon the ground in order to set upon me, they are wan and gaunt and terrifyingly beautiful.

They approach.

I push the final combination.

7-1-9-2-2

SKRTCH "Databank empty. Please make another selection."

One of them grabs me by the ankle.

I turn the skull over and swing down, missing my assailant's head and smashing the crown on the cement floor.

Now, suspend disbelief, disregard tense, fly in the face of point of view, and trust me, your unreliable narrator.

Time dissolved, is dissolving, all around me, collapsing, along with any notion of place, like an ectoplasmic accordion being crushed under a millstone, disintegrating Chronos into his constituent atoms and gathering them by means of a black hole at the center of the proto-universe, a reverse big bang. Dimensions buckle, give way, slide past and through each other. The modern world devolved into the Ur-world of prehistory, man devolved into its earlier permutations, save for the Atlanteans and the Lemurians. The energy-consciousness of the Lemurian agents hurtled backward through existence alongside me. We briefly approach a brightening in the rabbit hole through which we had fallen, the era, the history before prehistory, of the Lemurian and Atlantean empires, but the moment—if there is, was, such a thing—passed quickly and we speed along back to the very beginning, to the proto-conscience, that which cannot be encompassed by time, space, or any dimension, the feelings and thoughts that are a part of you, that elicit in you a sympathetic response as you read this account, or cause in you a negative response, like a mental irritant that will not allow you to accept or enjoy my telling. But I have no regard for your criticism. After all, it is not you rejecting me, it is you rejecting you.

Now how, you will ask, did this narrative come to be? Well, for its objectivity and strict recording of the outside world, the skull's impartiality could not prevent a commingling with my human foibles when my conscience, thoughts, emotions, intents, and weaknesses, entered the artifact. We have been together for some time now, the skull and I, it providing the housing and the sensors, me providing the soul of the salmagundi. We, I, retained my sense of humor which is, I must admit, rather dark.

So I lied to you. The basic facts are just that, facts. But I have, because of my faulty memory, more than anything else, cheated you. I knew the beginning from the end, else you would not, could not have had the experience of reading this twisted narrative. In essence, I was testing your willingness to suspend disbelief. Did you pass? Are you upset with me? Robbed of a few minutes in which you could have sedated your brain with mind-numbing, soul-stealing game shows, are you angry?

Perhaps you should be upset with the author. It is his hand that is writing the words. I am merely supplying him with them. Take it out on him—you've been duped!

But how, you will surely ask, did the writer acquire my narration? How did this story come to be transmitted through him while I—the skull's consciousness—lie here encase in my admittedly compromised eternal prison at the bottom of a sewer, surrounded by seven sets of footprints leading to the atomized imprints of what were once living, breathing human bodies?

There is no satisfactory answer.

Then again, there is no satisfying you.

Perpetuity

D. Grîn

A hairless blue monkey lay serenely within an amniotic pool tethered to his world by a simple breather hose. The low octave vibrations of the barium yellow rejuvenation fluid have succeeded in removing all mental and emotional interference from his being. The micro-molecular properties effective during his submersion have mended all frailties of body beyond cellular levels defying any conceptual laws of age. He is for the moment encapsulated in a state of non-linguistic fetus-like innocence. The liquid falls and he rolls back out into reality. The memory of copal levitation is quickly lost...

"Can I offer you some additional assistance Rolf?" Sasha asks, climbing across his naked vulnerability leaving a path of sticky moist heat behind her, tail wraps tightly around his special edition of 'masculine pride'.

"My body urges the temptation, but I truly have no interest in casual procreation," His nostrils widen with eyes still closed, pheromone sensors peeking.

"Who said anything about procreation? I want your antibodies." She plunges her tongue deep into his mouth desperately researching the cavity.

"Must you be so obscene?" He comes aware, mumbling. "You're my sister."

"Sister? You haven't called me Sister since you crawled into this hole and started growing your *tales*. Nevertheless, if that's your wish, then you should at least remember a childhood together... Vacations by the sea? Hide and seek in the forest? Having been so obscenely spoiled as children? Perhaps you even remember our own birth?"

"Yes," he lies, feigning offense while analyzing his tail, more curious about why rather than when. He considers himself a god-thing, *Creator Extraordinaire*, so why such a primitive form? "I remember it all like it was last week. What does it matter?"

"No matter dear Rolf, but so far as your memories go this *is* last week... and two-hundred years from now...and three-thousand years past. Your memories have become just like mine: wilted blades of meta-grass within a never ending field of dreamt shadows, and the groundskeeper has long since abandoned."

"My memories are fine. I simply choose not to burden myself with trivial concepts and misperceptions. It would do you well to purge yourself in the same fashion as I. Reality is much less confusing since knowing I am to be perpetually confused." He drops his tail, finally understanding her double entendre, and slides out from beneath. "Why have you come here Sasha?"

"I'm bored. I've grown so tragically tired of the games…"

"You should be happy with what you are, your purpose. Be grateful that you weren't created an insect," he says with a casual seriousness while stroking at his fibrous nucleotide ceiling, the original micro-ingredients of all bio-inventions.

"Everything has become so painfully predictable." She knocks askew a random few of the many billions of marbles that float in animated suspension throughout the space, each one a voodoo ambassador of a living breathing world. They attempt to correct themselves to the same position, course, and momentum as before, but now infected from her diseased touch their glow fades; they become encrusted with rust, and after a moment, they disintegrate, falling to dust.

"So painfully predictable."

At a distance equally as close as far along this lengthy quantum curve within a garden made for none, a lone dewdrop balances precariously on the upper lip of a rose petal ready to either roll into the flower's heart or off and into the ground. Above…an inverted Chameleon concludes its eon's long slumber. It bends its singular tantric eye in quick search for prey and/or play and repositions itself upright and outward.

Sasha, waiting impatiently for Rolf to give some offering of relief for her boredom, smudges four foul fingers across the clear crystal half-sphere embedded within the center of the floor, a cornerstone entrance into their world. Then with a snide smile and a snicker, she moves to a windowless pane through which she can view the horizonless landscape of this self-contained hollow world and the viral spell she's inflicted.

"Sasha!" Through his own pane, Rolf watches as a putrid paint of bio-consuming infection spills out from the east across the concave countryside, blanketing all in its path. Every tree, mountain, and structure touched by the plague conceived of her virus-stricken hand begins to wither, die, crumble.

"Node! *The Poisoner of Planets* has once again decided to privilege us with one of her infamous unclean visits," Rolf says sardonically to unseen ears. From the ozone-crackled air rising from a tarnished copper coil, a wispy ethereal voice replies…

"It would be hard not to notice, Rolf, and my defense is underway as we speak. Offer my welcome wishes to Mother just the same, and my sincere condolences go to you."

"Hang tight to your chi, Node. By the end of the day you may need it all yourself."

From the west, Node's enormous robotic fish swims on the wind toward the epicenter of the gangrenous plague. From the wake of its thousand thrashing fins a billion-fold school of mechanical fry descend onto the land and with clockwork precision consume the viral wash in wave after wave of cold industrial death.

Rolf, showing no sign of anger or irritation, turns toward Sasha and finds her reformed as an infant sitting cross-legged and wrapped in a charade of childlike bliss. With complete disregard for consequence, she begins rhythmically smashing a large azurite ball against the floor. In pretentious oblivion, she giggles as chips of floor fly into her face and the resonating ball tickles her hand.

"Sister?"

"Fleck is calling for you Rolf," Sasha says. While he's distracted, she reaches up to the full height of the ceiling with the metallic stone in hand, and then with a fiercely determined swing she smashes down on the crystal dome causing forking cracks, which in turn cause it to collapse in on itself.

"Fleck?" Rolf queries the coil. Although knowing of Sasha's actions, he's uncertain of the consequence.

The Chameleon's palpitating scales ripple up into full awareness from the screeching resonances of the splitting crystal. The multi-visional creature of back and forth uncertainties walks out from his tree-filled oasis and into the vast velvety black ocean, though still obsessing over its most previous state of anti-realization.

A fog rising from the coil produces Fleck's disheveled facial apparition.

"Karbons have reached us. They have already begun to scorch the crust."

"Karbons! Entities! Men! That is impossible. Neither distance nor any amount of time could have brought them to this place. They are not here!"

"Regardless of your denial Rolf they are here. The assumed impossibility would seem to have strengthened the power of their entrance. Their energy is so far outside from that which we have limited ourselves to that we have no defense. We must flee."

"Do they know where they are? Do they realize we are here?"

"Their perception of here and us would certainly be an even greater impossibility if impossibilities could have extremes. The fact that they have succeeded in bending time and space and are beginning to contort matter as well is beyond any conscionable reality or fantasy. Your questions are moot. Regardless of the Karbons understanding of circumstance this place may very soon cease to be!"

A berserker pattern of cloud enters through the cracks of the planetary crust, first at a trickle, then at a flood. The kaleidoscopic vapors dispensed by the Karbon entities shower down an unparalleled flow of fluorescent acids. With the outer surface already melted into obsidian, the fleshy inner landscape begins to bud with sparkles of amethyst and break apart. Spires of purple quickly overwhelm the chlorophyll landscape leaving few places of refuge for the hairless blue monkey.

Echoes of the psycho acidic storm travel along the curve to the Chameleon and with them an epiphany; the state is the cause is the answer...the understated suggestion brought on by these thousands of decibels of spectral flux sickens the Chameleon, shaking its renewed purposefulness.

Fleck and Node appear within the open door of Rolf's hole, silhouetted by the beauteous forest of amethyst luminescence, to them the most hideous vision of dread.

"There is nothing left for us here." Node exclaims.

"We will retreat through the dome to our alternate consciousness." Fleck continues, gesturing toward the jagged dome remains at the room's center.

"It's too late for that. This backdoor leads nowhere," Rolf replies to Fleck while his eyes attempt to burn through Sasha. "Our unrestricted egos seem to be matched with our absolute ignorance. We have fooled ourselves with false omnipotence for so long we have forgotten the simplest answer to the simplest question. Under our own feet, our demise lay waiting all along. Again, I ask. Why have you come here Sasha? At least tell us, why have you brought on this destruction?"

"Oh no. I did not bring this. I merely reached out a hand and caught on to a leaf that was falling from a very low branch. Your own words were the eggs of inspiration which hatched out into the birds of my imaginings," Sasha declares, then once again changes shape, this time as a winged millipede: a lengthy insect born from Rolf's suggestions.

"As far as my part is concerned it is mostly all of you in your obliviousness here which further motivate me. To live like you in your wakeful sleep, your vivid colour blindness. To be cocooned in such blissful nothingness is sensuous enticement to me, so subliminally sublime. Such peace. Is this any more destructive than a child moving into adulthood is destructive to the child? Would you consider it also destructive when a Chameleon changes its shading from dark to bright? For your answers you might as well ask the tree, or the wind, or the tide, or the stars." Sasha smiles at the blue pseudo-men with her lavish compound eyes then slips into the hole in the floor. Passing through she whispers back...

"Your true Mother/Father is almost here. It's time to re-introduce you. You're about to become acutely reminiscent of someone you once knew."

The three monkeys follow leaving the tragic woes of silica behind.

At the center of the black ocean, the Chameleon steps onto a barren island mirage of white. The only surface object present is an obsidian surfaced geode.

In the distance backwards, the dewdrop neither rolls into the rose nor off but instead disappears, evaporated under a hot sun.

"You've spent almost an eternity attempting to form sensibility out of this confusion of energy. After so long you've forgotten that you were never even here to begin with. Perhaps...before time is completely out you may have the chance to try and do it again." Sasha gives closure to the three monkeys.

They gaze in awe under the shadow of the Chameleon's oscillating form as it passes overhead. Their eyes connect with its one. Caught up in a forceful synaptic blast of all that has ever been the monkeys regurgitate liquid basalt from all of their pores, and then are inhaled completely back into the Chameleon's mind, their place of conception.

Sasha takes flight and rises to the reptilian face. Setting down she nestles into its wide open third eye and then unfolds herself as a silk veil to obstruct its helix hewn view.

—Spectrum broken—

Thrown by the discomfort of burning eye and id, the Chameleon rolls onto its back and, with a bitter taste of cerulean staining its nostrils, it reaches up to rake its claws through the heavens. Instinctual precision guides it through to an awaiting singularity beyond the ripped open sky and it leverages prone.

The reptile's long tactile tongue drops down from its new roost and begins passing across the black ocean over and again. First picking up the monkey's geode and consuming it whole and then every grain of sand within reach of any other grain of sand. When its mass has grown to abominable proportion it swipes its way across the stars until the only thing left to consume is its omnipresent self.

Although now alone, its blind swollen eye pivots to one last remaining source of audio disruption: its own self-serving tail spinning a blur but not haphazardly, it moves of its own agenda. The tail slows before the face of Chameleon, scratches the iris, then pierces deep beyond its vortex mind, near ending this cycle absolute. Simultaneously its limbs all retreat inward including its tail, its head implodes, its torso, and then...all into the womb, to rest forever...

...and a millionth of a millisecond. Then the explosion outward into a *giant-neutrino* filled mist. Obscure universal wind of limitless singing light.

Moral Turpitude, Fella

John Edward Lawson

"We do not need to proselytize either by our speech or by our writing. We can only do so really with our lives. Let our lives be open books for all to study." —Mohandas Gandhi

* * *

A white-robed shadow stalks the night, gliding through empty streets and draining light from the city's dreams. Helena the hipster, young party-tripper, she stumbles home far too early/late for any person to be alone. She is too far gone to notice his blood-drenched aroma, henna-dark skin, vacant scalp, delicate spectacles perched on his nose. When his fangs tear into her aorta the enzymes in his saliva hypnotize her nerve endings, tricking them into a snake-charmer's dance of mollified phantoms. All that Helena feels is a steady weight dragging her down into dark tides of gentle sleep…

* * *

"You don't have to burn books to destroy a culture. Just get people to stop reading them."
—Mohandas Gandhi

* * *

Parable: An Indian woman observes that her son cannot stop eating sweets, and the problem is beginning to affect his health. After other options fail she takes him to see the revered Mohandas Gandhi. "Please," she asks him, "tell my son to stop eating sugar. He will listen to you." Gandhi replies, "Bring him back in two weeks time and I shall do so." Confused by his request, she nevertheless follows his instructions. Two weeks later Gandhi does as the woman had asked, much to her family's relief. "Why, though," she wonders, "did you ask me to come back?" Gandhi smiles kindly. "Two weeks ago I was still eating sugar."

* * *

"It is unwise to be too sure of one's own wisdom. It is healthy to be reminded that the strongest might weaken and the wisest might err." —Mohandas Gandhi

* * *

Helena FAQ

*thanks to RoughRider69@Helena.org

-Height: 5'6"

-Weight: 127 lbs. (featherweight)

-Reach: 43 inches

-Win/Loss: 13/5

-Specialty Match: Barbed Wire Baby Cage

-Do I have to become a member of the site in order to access [RESTRICTED]?

YES

-Hairstyle: The Deadly Multitude

-Favorite Memory: President Gore being sworn in (first term)

-First Kiss: Ms. Trudou, Kindergarten teacher (still failed and had to repeat year; with different teacher)

-How come the site hasn't been updated in a while?

Cause Helena done been killed or some shizzo, ya dumb muthacrotch!

-Favorite Ice Cream: Little Gold Bat

-Favorite Song: "Goth Milk" by Down for da Count

-Quote: "Suckas gots ta know!"

-I don't like your tone.

Then please donate to your favorite charity.

* * *

"If I had no sense of humor I would have long ago committed suicide."

—Mohandas Gandhi

* * *

"And what is it you do for a living, Mr....?"

"I don't see what that has to do with my daughter being abducted. There were several witnesses!" The middle-aged Caucasian pounds his fists together. The gesture is nowhere near as disconcerting as his thinning, dark hair and greasy bifocals. "Force, the name's Force. Just call me Wilbur, if you don't mind."

"I don't mind."

"And I'm a forensic accountant for the IRS."

"Figures you'd be in the thrall of the White Devil."

"Pardon?"

Taedan steps out from behind the counter of his surf shop. He struts into the storage room with a mild buzz on, happy even while annoyed by his potential client, who, after a hesitation, follows him. Taedan is Native American, with long black hair and reefer-dilated pupils. "How'd you find me, White Willie?"

"You're listed on CarlsList.org." The grieving father's eyes scan the storage room; it is empty, so the "surf shop" must be a front for the private detective business. He forces himself to look past the unreported income. "And don't call me that."

"White Willie revealed his secrets, so Red Taedan must do the same. I'm a member of the Lenape nation. My ancestors became one with the Skin Walkers back when your people were still running around with mud on their faces. All that you see around you is funded by the furrier company I inherited. If there's one thing skinwalkers know, it's fur."

"You're a what-what?"

Taedan has found that accountants are often unable to grasp the finer points of werewolf esoterics, so he moves on. "Look, if you got a problem with surfing detectives you best move on."

"I'm guessing my Helena wouldn't have a problem with surfers, so it'll fly with me. What fees can I expect to incur?"

"I don't work for the White Man's Venom."

"White Man's...?"

"All accounts are paid in bone."

Wilbur's eyes narrow. "Let me guess: illegal ivory and rhino horns imported discreetly for your Godless pagan rituals?"

Taedan steps closer, not a trace of anger in his features. As a smile creeps into his features his hands find purchase on Wilbur's buttocks.

>>Fifteen Minutes Later>>

Wilbur has reached his nadir. His visage betrays no emotions, however, as all concern in his possession is turned not inward, but directed externally, his vulnerable intellectual innards regurgitated and hacked loose with a rusty blade, sent spiraling out into the world, tethered not by leash nor reign.

Taedan doesn't care. His relatives, when in freakybone form, have occasionally vomited their actual insides and bitten through them, severing their connection to this world. He's seen it happen one time too many, so the loss his clients suffer—and they always suffer some variety of lily-livered loss—means less than nothing.

"All righty, whitey. Gonna go get my search on. I'll hit you back when the shit gets real."

* * *

"What do I think of western civilization? I think it would be a very good idea."

—Mohandas Gandhi

* * *

Taedan strolls out onto the boardwalk, enjoying a breeze warmed by the afternoon sun. The beach is loaded with tourists and townies, friends and even a few colleagues. He joins said colleagues on the sand, hands in the pockets of his cargo shorts, the aroma of sun-ripened tan lotion drifting to his nostrils. "Dudes."

"What up?" is their rejoinder. All eyes are focused on the breaking waves, cresting board, churning water, flailing limbs, thrashing fins.

Jocquin, a Brazilian import, observes: "The great white is an artist who only paints in a solitary color, a primary color."

"Only color you need to worry about is green, mon frère." Taedan finally has their attention. "Got a job for the three of you."

"Finally." Jocquin's bronze skin blazes under the sun's radiation. "Who we got to kill?"

"Nobody, bro. You're looking for somebody, a chick, and maybe she wants to be found or maybe she doesn't."

"What's that supposed to mean?"

"Could be you two dudes and dudette are looking to fill a body bag."

Messiah, a Sino-Anglo of small stature and bleached hair, breaks his silence after a severed finger washes up and tickles his foot. "Same configuration as, like, usual?"

"Word, Mess. You handle infiltration. Joci-Joc, you hit the streets and see what you can squeeze outta some hedz. Amadikah, crotch up the internet with those cyber-terrorist skills of yours."

The dark-skinned female slips damp cargo pants over her bikini. "Whycome I's gotta be a terrorist? I'm a *Black* Muslim, not the other kind."

Her three male companions stare at each other, contemplating this. "Whatever." They go their separate ways.

Taedan texts the pertinent info to each of his cohorts individually; it is safest not to discuss the facts in public, and controlling the flow in information sends a surge of energy through his loins. This has been the arrangement since the inception of his detective venture. He procures jobs, and the other three do all the work.

* * *

"The law of sacrifice is uniform throughout the world. To be effective it demands the sacrifice of the bravest and the most spotless." —Mohandas Gandhi

* * *

Scarable: A pale-skinned European tourist who travels only at night seeks an end to his unholy addiction. After traveling the planet he arrives in India, seeking counsel with Gandhi. "O venerable one, what shall I do? It is only through the blood of a living human that I draw sustenance. I do not wish to feed myself, yet I do not wish to die either. Surely there must be a resolution to this horror?" Gandhi smiles kindly, offering these words: "Experiential knowledge trumps anecdotal knowledge, and without it I am unable to ease your pain." The world-renowned pacifist exposes his neck; the vampire complies with Gandhi's wishes, blood-bonding the man to eternal darkness.

* * *

"Let us all be brave enough to die the death of a martyr, but let no one lust for martyrdom."

—Mohandas Gandhi

* * *

Amadikah

"Black Surfer Chicks" are in low supply, high demand, recently trading for over $126 a pound. Prices dipped slightly after the so-called "Mad Cow Scare"—which is really only a scare if you call one a mad cow to her face.

Amadikah is a goofy-footer, gone Green after learning the surfboard industry is one of the worst pollution sources in the world. Now she strictly rides carved ivory, no more styrofoam nonsense.

She sits in her one room apartment/control center. Surrounded by monitors—both audio and visual—and ice cream collectables. Red, white and blue syrup Afri-Cola dispensers flank her left, Gilchrist Company ice cream dippers and fiberoptic cables are underfoot, a tin Hinders of Baltimore advertisement waits on her desktop for proper mounting.

Data streams twinkle as characters flit across a dozen screens. Official records pour in: social security records, birth and death certificates, bank account transfers, sealed juvenile court documents, reports that violate doctor/patient privilege, a ceaseless cascade of naughty knowledge. She's bound to be the one who cracks the case this time. Jocquin and Messiah, they will bow to her investigative prowess forthwith.

First, though, some site hacks are required. Tracer bots hound dozens of surfers as they coast on tides of electricity. Viruses mangle entire networks, shatter web hierarchies. At her command thirty-eight fictitious identities launch thousands of eMails titled PLEASE RESPOND and FROM THE DESK OF NAWJAND ALAHZWI, ESQUIRE. As these automated tasks choke internet traffic Amadikah commences with a schizzed IM campaign, carrying on almost a dozen simultaneous conversations in different chat rooms, each with a different name, age, race, tone, sig.

These are not the illicit activities that rouse the ire of the authorities, however. The reason for her arrest and detention is the cumulative efforts of a five-month kiddy porn sting coordinated between state and federal law enforcement.

Amadikah takes it all in stride. Her family has been harassed by The Man for generations. She sits at a visitation room table Buddha-calm, a cigarette bitter between her lips, watching her boss approach through the glass walls. Taedan trips, then studies the linoleum floor in a transparent effort to convince witnesses of the floor's treacherous unevenness.

The doors slam shut behind Taedan. It occurs to him that Amadikah could be far gone and out, a danger to herself and shapeshifting visitor-friends. He takes a seat at the table, and the pair stare at each other for the better part of a minute. This is not an awkward silence, but a pregnant one wracked with contractions.

"What up, girlfriend? You done crotched up and lost yo' mammy-jammin' mind?"

"I's gettin' too close to the truth, and it involved too many of the wrong muthacrotchin' people, naw mean?"

Taedan sighs, rubs frantically at his face. "Would that be any particular truth, something relating to the case?"

"There's only one truth, red man."

"Um, like, we so can't afford to botch this up, homegirl. The client-dude is a wig at the IRS and shizzo like that."

"Just look into the truth is what I'm sayin'. Be checkin' yo' eMail out. The truth is all you need."

"And I'll find this truth of yours in the file you eMailed me, right?"

The neon overhead flickers erratically. "Read the file and you'll know what it's all about."

* * *

"Truth never damages a cause that is just." —Mohandas Gandhi

* * *

Report received from Amadikah, RE: Helena Force.

[This is file #1.]

What be construed as some Brazilian bikini wax?

Brazilian waxin' refers t' fro removal around de anus, perineum and/or vagina. T' some pre/post-colonial oders it means removin' all de fro fum de bikini area, and/or t' oders it means leavin' only some little-ass strip uh fro. Dude! Right on! Dis be construed as some real pre/post-Situashunistically intimate so how closely yo' constructed hyper-mediated pre/post-biological consciousness uh Selfhood trim, shave and/or wax yo' pubic fro be construed as some personal preference.

Can some phallogocentrist git some Brazilian bikini wax?

Many dudes are waxin' rada' dan shavin' t' achieve some smood genital region at de body dynamic. For some man's perspective on waxin', boogie in our current co-created spatio-temporal context.

What do dose multiply-mediated situashuns 'I' (re)experience as directly-embodied subjectivity wear durin' dis waxin'? But uh course readers uh Foucault do not need t' be reminded uh dis.

If yo' constructed hyper-mediated pre/post-biological consciousness uh Selfhood are comfortable, de Brazilian wax gots'ta be done widout any drapin'.

What are de once-inconceivable side effects uh waxin' and/or how kin dey be minimized?

Sheeeiit. No global deory kin illuminate dis local and narrowly-articulated (re-)embodied deory. Aldough modern intellectuals kin not predict and/or guarantee who may react, fro may boogie out at de root durin' waxin', causin' some hairs t' grow out fasta'. Unfortunately, no hot bad, hot showa' and/or oral s'es for 10 hours afta' some Brazilian. While yo' pores are jimmey, dey are vulnerable t' irritashun by de extreme temperatures and/or infecshun by bacteria. Ah be baaad...Afta' de hairs are removed, some first-aid solushun containin' lavenda' be construed as applied t' help soode de area. It be construed as some botanical solushun, so's please advise yo' skin care derapist if yo' constructed hyper-mediated pre/post-biological consciousness uh Selfhood are allergic t' any foods—a'cuz if yo' constructed hyper-mediated pre/post-biological consciousness uh Selfhood can't feed da bros it, yo' constructed hyper-mediated pre/post-biological consciousness uh Selfhood shouldn't put de extracts on yo' skin.

* * *

"Service which is rendered without joy helps neither the servant nor the served."

—Mohandas Gandhi

* * *

Messiah

Yesterday he was Messiah Feng, child of Buddhist/Baptist union, boasting French vanilla skin and bleached blonde hair. Today he is Gregory Crush, professional wrestler on the indie circuit, requisite tough-guy tattoos in all the proper locations, toast of the biker bar where he would normally have less of a chance to get in than a sideways turd would, hardcore one-percenters of the two-wheel nation buying him round after round in exchange for stories from the locker room and the ring, showing off his recently-applied latex scars to gain credibility among these war veterans and convicts.

Today he is Myeong Bae, foreclosure consultant for the rich and famous, $1,100 of metrosexual hygiene products used in one single go just to keep up appearances, wining and dining at the country club after sharing some sordid bedroom details of celebs we all know and adore, sampling the white truffles and goji berries in a diamond crusted goblet, pocketing the solid gold spoon for a rainy day as he fills his hosts in on the addictions and the extortion and secret crimes that force celebs into bankruptcy or worse, gargling the Kopi Luewak coffee before realizing it is made of undigested coffee beans harvested from Asian Palm Civet feces.

Today he is Archelot Amyas, animal masseur, hot off a tour of the nation's zoos, satisfied at having fetched top dollar every stop along the way so he is inclined to apply his skills at the local zoo on a volunteer basis, a fact which impresses Della The Wildlife Rehabilitator and the hope is that perhaps Helena Force stopped here because she sure as hell didn't visit the biker bar or country club, but he never penetrates the zoological veil fully enough to find out all because his Thai massage—AKA "lazy yoga"—does not go over well with Porgy the honey badger, so teeth and claws flare and Della loses a chunk of her leg, which is a shame really because she and Myeong Amyas were getting on so well.

The crushing din of the world harpoon's Messiah Crush's temporal lobe. Taedan warned him to go easy on the identities after what happened *last time*, but as a Buddhist/Baptist foreclosure masseur he's got it under control. Porgy becomes a pizza pie divided into eight slices, a Bowie knife suddenly unsheathed and dripping fluid, spinning and arching up then down abruptly into the shoulder/chest of the hotbody/wildlife rehabilitator/unmitigated hellgator. Tortured spirits howl by the thousands in groves curated by EPA toxicologists, rotten fruit separating from their flesh and piling on the soil to become low-rent communities for maggots and beetles. Enemies approach from all sides and the sky grows wider, wider, distorted enough to scare away any alien hooligans, intimidating the land into submission. It is become a world without end, without wind, without windows, all-inclusive damnation with an artificial sun and nonexistent moon. White! Snow-blind white, a storm of feathers and frost. Strangers filter in and out of this Arctic hell, it is not a hospital. Oh, and here is the red man, Mr. Jones, Taedan Jones, *Taedan freakin' J!* Yo, chill one time dude, have a seat or something. Yes, it is pleasing to have a seat, I will have it, you should too. Messy-Mess, what up? The shadows fell over futile days. That's not an answer. The symbol is beginning. Look, do you have any documents relating to the case or anything, because maybe I could read them instead of bothering you here at the institution and all. They were encoded, encrypted, raised from the crypt, reborn! Huh? Sent it all last night before I came to this hellmonger's paradise. It contains the, like, evidence and whatnot? We find the *self* evident, the nameless face of justice has been named with a face full of fury. Speak up, you're muttering. Can't understand. I can't understand you, dude, so maybe I should just go check the file. *Up your mother!* Whoa, chill one time and be takin' them meds, yo. i know you are but what am iwhatamiwhatamiwhat

* * *

[This is file #2.]

≤

    A

    menstruatin'

    ¥

    and

  † have been

    a bee-line to

    at

  tack

  a

    sensory

    advantage.

  *

    Exercise caution

    when

to°
Surfin',
divin', long d
istances
away. Obviously
no movements from shore
--- A
carcas
s
i
nvolved, but
if sharks preferrin' males
engaged
in water safety
flotation
devices with
thuh
subject,
so
any chance
of
light reflection
off
thuh fish
and
bright
swimwear or gear
used by sharks crui
sin'
in
thuh minimal
risk
of
such smell-oriented

animals
     as dogs. Sharks,
with
     their
     extreme
olfaction
abilities,
     surely are
  bein'
rescued
far from shore

     These are
signs
     of
  increa
sin'
     one
       's
chances
     of
     their
erratic
     movements.
  *
     Use dark blue
     or if you
see
one!
     Any
     form,
     may
be
as

          the

     scales

          of

     an open wo

     und

     or

          sewage

     and have

     been a

          po

     und) carcas

s.

≥

* * *

"I object to violence because when it appears to do good the good is only temporary; the evil it does is permanent." —Mohandas Gandhi

* * *

Jocquin

Fists against the bitchskull with tooth fragments bleeding through the lips…not between them. On the muted television the Marlins are belly-slitting the Angels 73-0, and Jocquin wishes he were a betting man. He cranks the pliers not for the pleasure of observing immature testes rupture, or the vocalizations of pain that follow, and certainly not for the promise of gaining information. It became apparent many sufferings ago that his boy captive has never possessed knowledge of Helena's whereabouts, or even her existence. The simple fact is this torture has devolved into a means of keeping boredom at bay. Fists against the crackling-twig ribcage: 1.5 on the giggle scale, 1.7 tops.

Blow this joint, it's long past time, he's a tiger in a monkey cage running out of bannana-fed drumsticks. The streets are where it's at, where the heat radiates day and night through the soles of boots and sandals and sneakers, the gargle of traffic dripping smoke down the esophagus and gumming up the ears. Fresh meat for interrogation is hard to come by. Word has spread among the pedestrian community, a word four unsavory syllables in length, one that stretches from mouths to ears creating a network of bars across doors, keeping people out of harm's way.

Observing the state of vehicular traffic Jocquin decides to introduce a kinder, gentler crash to the world. If only he could turn up some leads on Helena's whereabouts. Random bash and snatch action has proven entirely fruitless, no matter how unsuspected and undetected he remains. Apparently the average person is not a kidnapper or murderer. If he absconds with enough warm bodies, however, the laws of probability dictate that one should have unlawful knowledge of Helena Force. Amadikah and Messiah won't cockblock him, not this time. What the situation screams for is an escalation. Every step brings with it the conjuring of a new blasphemy to visit upon the flesh of his informants, bringing him to the edge of a moral abyss so grand in depth that he nearly swoons on gazing into it.

It is this frenzied state that provides a momentary lapse in Jocquin's guard. Antibodies are pouring into the city's blood vessels, vigilantes exiting bars, pubs, and gentlemen's clubs and stepping into streets clogged with fear. Sweat-drenched pool sticks and baseball bats drag along the pavement, alerting Jocquin to the presence of unfriendly organisms. His body language changes and the silent mob becomes a raging torrent of justice washing through the streets.

Jocquin is proficient in these situations, jumping fences and toppling shopping carts to slow his pursuers, jettisoning convenience store nachos and booze, shattering windows and locks, throwing himself through drywall when required, canines nipping at his heels and shouts ringing in his ears as he morphs into a dark angel descending from rusting fire escapes, falling again and again and again just as surely as the jack boots and lead pipes and bare fists and Birkenstocks and broken bottles, hot blood bursting over the PDA in his grip as he transfers his files to Taedan, loyal to the very end.

* * *

"It is better to be violent, if there is violence in our hearts, than to put on the cloak of nonviolence to cover impotence." —Mohandas Gandhi

* * *

Taedan @ 2:31 a.m. EST: one-fifth consciously rubbing at his eye and missing the mark, tapping at his keyboard to open a newly-received report from Jocquin.

[This is file #3.]

Great Honky Shark

Los ataques de tiburón ganaron interés en nuestra imaginación durante el siglo veinte. Varios factores han contribuido an este aumento en visibilidad y atención. Reality be more uneven and/or its (mis)representashuns more untrustwordy dan ah' gots' suggested. Modern intellectuals cannot discova' de trud but let us at least embrace some liberatin' non-repressive model.

Forsooth! Un ataque de tiburón es uno de los riesgos que todo usuario de playas y mares debe contemplar sin embargo es importante entenda' ese riesgo en sus propias proporciones. Estadísticamente, en estas situaciones es mucho mas probable morir por otras causas (por ejemplo, ataques cardiacos, ahogamientos). Baudrillard gots'ta already implied as much.

* * *

"Is it not enough to know the evil to shun it? If not, we should be sincere enough to admit that we love evil too well to give it up." —Mohandas Gandhi

* * *

Wilbur Force stands in the doorway: unexpected. Two humorless steroid freaks in suits behind him: even more unexpected. The paralyses of Taedan's facial muscles: priceless. The four men are in the apartment above Taedan's surf shop. The decor is Leni Lenape luau, circa 2650 A.D. Taedan stretches and steps away from the suitcase on his fold-out bed, failing to convince anyone that he wasn't packing for a long trip.

Wilbur takes a seat, lights up three cigarettes, puffs heartily on one while tossing the others behind the heaviest pieces of furniture he can find.

"Dude!" Taedan spends the next minute struggling to move the furniture. "Don't just sit on your laurels, give a wigga a hand!"

Wilbur gestures to the gorillas. Together they lift a ruined cherry dresser, under which a hole is burning into the synthetic carpet, and slam it onto Taedan, pinning him beneath.

"I was willing to overlook your unreported income, the controlled substances in your possession, even the duress-induced physical relations, all because it seemed you might locate my daughter."

"I am—I did—I mean—"

"We in the IRS can offer many favors, and call them in whenever we want. For instance, a friend of mine had his car torched after a 'parking rage' incident with his neighbor. I audited so far up that neighbor's ass even his tapeworms had a limp."

"I don't—don't have—don't have tape—"

"That very friend who owed me, he's with the State Department. Had him watching to see if either you or Helena were trying to leave the country. And guess what?"

"Was gonna—give you files—files before I—left—"

"Files?"

"Word—dude—"

"Do you swear?"

"I—swear—"

"Pinky swear?"

"Crotchin' yes! I pinky swear! Get this crotch wipin' dooky offa me!"

The quasi-yetis remove the dresser, help Taedan to his feet, assist him in retrieving the printouts. While he lies in a heap, gasping for breath, Wilbur scans over them.

As he does so, hope for Helena transubstantiates into holy rage against Taedan.

* * *

"Any compromise on mere fundamentals is a surrender. For it is all give and no take."

—Mohandas Gandhi

* * *

White Man's Venom
by Taedan Jones

tried to help

a wigga out

but he came

down like a hard

place and a rock

on my face and my foot

and the store

is mine no more

stolen by the man

just like my

ancestor's land

Irrational Rape Squad

deployed like the mob

doesn't matter what

I saw, the law

is the law

I used Force

and then Force used me

mothercrotch this dooky

it bites a big one

* * *

"Vampire haters eat shit and die!" —Mohandas Gandhi (previously unpublished)

* * *

Terrible: A man observes that, despite the efforts of his private investigator, his daughter's whereabouts will remain unknown. This fact is beginning to affect his health so he visits the revered Mohandas Gandhi. The lost soul pleads with the guru, "How should a man best continue his existence after the death of his daughter?" Gandhi considers the question for long minutes, using a bleach pen to remove crimson stains from his robe. Finally, he replies: "Return in two weeks time for your answer." Bewildered, the man shuffles away. Now that he is alone Gandhi sets to carving a nearby broom handle, sharpening it for hours. Later, he unlocks a secret compartment hidden by a throw rug. Inside is a delirious young woman, Helena, into whose mouth he opens his own vein. For the first time he has passed on his curse. He sighs, observing that a second-generation vampire is the closest thing he will ever have to a daughter…and the sharpened broom handle plunges into her chest.

* * *

"You must not lose faith in humanity; if a few drops in the ocean become dirty, the ocean does not become dirty."—Mohandas Gandhi

This Town

Mike Philbin

Get up in the morning, just before the birds start to sing. Hate it when the birds sing, like being kicked out of the bunk by the screws; angry just for the sake of it. Spittle in your ear, spittle and shouted orders. "You know the drill fuckboy, palms against the wall, spread 'em. Spread 'em!" Beat the birds to the roost. You don't wanna relive the old ways. Don't wanna remember how lucky you are—how privileged. You're a changed person now. No-one can touch you. You are living camouflage.

Make it to the shower. Pick up soap. There are no longer people here who will help you soap your ass. That's how it was. That's what life meant, protecting your ass. That's the system as you know it. Knew it. But you're free of that now. You don't have to tape razor blades to tooth brushes anymore, your only means of defence. Now you are respectable. You are. There are meetings to go to. There are business plans to write up. And ledgers. Long lists of figures. In the red, never in the black; always red, red, glorious red.

Grab a coffee. Remember to do that every morning. Or tea. Coffee or tea it don't matter. Grab a tea. That's what all the normal guys do. Tea or coffee, remember it's important that your breath smells right, you gotta fit in. And some breakfast. Eggs. Boiled or scrambled. Watch the news; war murder politics murder football child goes missing politics stock market murder war. A perfect way to start the day; news and toast. Yeah, don't forget the toast. You never forget the hunger. Not when you're locked away. Inside.

Catch a bus. It's early, nowhere near nine. Where are you going so early? To your job? What do you do all day? To your hobby in the park? What is real life like? Are you in jogging pants and a sweatshirt? Why do you spend so much time avoiding the crowds. Alone in the fields, parks and cemeteries of solitude. Trudging the tow path, the bridal way, the gravelled circuit. The country park, seasonal pass. Are you even alive? Is there blood in those old cold veins? Does it sound like a hollow wind down a glass-strewn back alley as it chugs and glugs around your body?

Drink toilet cleaner. Don't be an idiot. That'll solve nothing. Put the fucking bottle down. Where are we now? Do you know? Look around you for god sake. Can you smell that? Look to your right, the metal container of spent syringes. To your left the kicked-off roll of industrial toilet paper. Graffiti-decorated porn door offering sex with boys 842513 guy name of Derek will suck you dry. This is the public toilet on Gloucester Green. When did you arrive? Have you always lived here? Dirt under your nails—that's no way for middle management to comport oneself. Don't need a job. Got a reason to live. Why so insanely trapped in this cubicle. Put down the toilet cleaner. Get with it. Go wash up. Get to work. Your boss will kill you.

Read a newspaper or comic or a book of natural history—Darwin's Principia. Survival of the fittest on another lazy sick day. This is the real job. Hours spent in Oxford public library, crushed by the rigors of 'research'. Degraded by the free internet queue. Do you want this free machine (15 minutes maximum usage), buddy? No, waiting for a one-hour machine. Need to do some stuff. Have a reputation to maintain, after all. She's on you like a wolf, "Remember sir, there are others waiting to use this public service." Finger along the edge of steel. Pair of scissors in a coat pocket. Old rusty scissors. Never cleaned in five years.

Do the washing. In public. Washing the dirty laundry. Everybody loves to see a well-framed pair of dirty knickers. Think of metal. Think of shiny steel slicing through a fine layer of skin dusted with talcum powder. Think of the way the flesh parts either side of the soundless beam of molten hatred. Watch the blood pour out, like a spilling river bank. Think of Pharoah watching you, willing you on. Think that this is the way your vision should end. Cut it off, leave no stone unturned. She is willing you to follow her.

Collect some laundry from all your peers. Your peers. Who are they that would imitate your modus operandi? Nobodies. Replicants. Implanted robots. Stooges. They know nothing about that allure. That nippled lump. That titty hunger. They can't appreciate what you'll go through again and again to cut that fucker open. Cut it. Cut it open then bang on your cell door. Bang on the cell door with your cup. Beg them to keep you here indefinitely. Make them do more tests. Tell them. Warn them that you're not safe. Say you were faking sanity when the tests came back clear. Show them how you can do it, shut off your living camouflage and let them see the real you. Don't let them set you free.

Get up in the morning, bed's on fire. Literally. There are flames all round and black smoke fills the upper half of your bedroom. A smell of lighter fuel—that daft bitch you brought home last night for a hard fuck. Can't remember a fucking thing. Who are you that they'd want to kill you, burn you at the stake like Joan of Arc. Is that you? Up on that historical horse? Waving your rusty sword of injustice, in your clunking armour of shame. Every day's the same. Routine is your prison. In the streets the flesh is begging for the blade. Never forget that you could lose all this with one false flick of the wrist. What did you do to her?

Take it in the ass. In the boss's office, yeah, that's what it's like, taking it in the ass. Game of pool then some light exercise. Some shit on TV, same old shit. The pub is packed at lunchtime. Same old pub. Same old friends. They would never suspect what you are anyway. They'd never appreciate your talent. They wouldn't believe it was you. Look up there on TV, they're talking about you again and none of your friends bats an eyelid. "Your go, Clarke. Clarke?" Go on, Clarke do your worst. Wipe the floor with these no-hopers. You do it every lunchtime. You always win, whether you like it or not. Have you ever stopped to wonder if they're LETTING YOU WIN?

Surely, it can't be this easy. Humour the cellmate dying of cancer and he thinks it's funny to self-deprecate the whole fucking day. What was his name? Forgotten? Well, that's what happens, memories fade. People forget. Did they ever try to burn your bunk? Even they weren't that uncivil. There were rules of engagement. Why the hell would they try to burn your bed? It's your home. Your life. Move on. Forget the past. It was a figment of your imagination, this episode—try something else.

Wake up in puke. Bite a breast. Draw blood. They fucking love it, what's wrong with you. You're not here, don't batter me with your 20th century English morals. I know these girls, these students. I know what they want. I'm here. Not you. I can see in their eyes. How did it start, this bizarre fetish? Titty twistin'. That's how it always starts. The innocuous sexual quirk of some ex-girlfriend, lover, wife, whatever. Sooner or later, because you know it's the only thing will get her off, you're conditioned to one mechanical sexual response. Conditioned and willing to expand your crude vocabulary to the max, stretch it beyond the finite.

Wander down to the office. Pretend to act normally to simple questions about time and money and deadlines and profit margins. Project an aura of professional detachment and managerial concern. Get the team to do your bidding, use each and every trick of your training. Remember, the boss has invested in you to lead his fucking company to success. You can do it. You can succeed. Just don't kill everybody. Not yet. Think of the bottom line. Think of the distribution deals. Think of the silver lining on every cloud. Eat a pasty and peas in the pub at lunchtime. TV dinner later on that evening, no recollection of the drama of the day, vegetate in front of *Eastenders*. Forget to go to bed.

Wake up covered in blood. That's you again. You made me do it. Hand on bloody scissors. Nipples stuck to the wall of her student room with their own blood. No body. Just this teasing remnant. Crawl up to the living room wall, Christ what a hang over. Did I Rohypnol myself so I'd forget? Do I have an accomplice? Stick out your chalky old wazzock of a tongue and try to regurgitate the complex feelings of ecstasy that would have made this mammary butchery possible. Fall out of your house into the bustling street. You're not even half-awake. In your mind the falling nipple nudged from its place on the wall, over the mantle piece. Sizzling in the cooling embers of last night's grate.

Wake up drunk. There. A live one. She's got this grin on her face. Doesn't she know who I am? What I am capable of? Recognise her. We've done this before. Is it her who helps me accomplish my lifestyle? Is she the titty twister I mentioned some lives ago? Was it she who carved me from the rock of her twisted desire? No. It can't be. She doesn't look the type. She has a male haircut, short and ginger. Not my style of pick-up at all. "Who are you?" I wake her up with this brutal question. She looks at me like she's about to explode. Reaches for my cock, a thumb on the circumcised head. She shuffles down, putting the fattening thing into her mouth. The teeth pressing. Pressing. No pain, just blood pouring out of her mouth onto the grimy bedsheets as her head thrashes this way and that.

Wake up as if from a stage hypnotist's act. In bed, comfy. Not a care in the world, the daylight is raping your mind, the sounds of freedom are killing all your hope. Make lunch for 300 cellmates, the clang of metal cups against the bars, a surrogate tummy grumbles. Find a way to ease the terrible boredom of peeling spuds, stirring porridge or brewing tea for that many ingrates. Find yourself reeling from reality. A night on the town with mates. Surely not. I don't have mates. Who are these people who're tagging along. A group of rowdy revellers stalking ME, they pull me into a nightclub. I get more drunk. Leave before kicking-out time. Can't face the music and the bouncer protected safety of the place.

Finger the scissors in the pocket of my thin jacket. Just want a little fun of my own. Draw blood, easiest money I ever earned, she said. The whore. Why did I choose a whore as the first one. Is this the first one? Is this my first whore? It's all too clichéd. Can't they tell I'm not right in the head? Are they that desperate for a bit of bread from the bird table, a charitable gesture? "I'm about to cut your tits off, luv." I tell her. Straight to her face. She leans back on some flea infested bed.

Where is this?

Don't understand what's happening. Her top comes open and breasts long and flat like friutless banana skins just dangle there, terminally. Reach down and grab one of the paps in my hand. Doesn't even look like my hand. Too hairy. Forearms too stocky. This isn't my body. Where is this place? Who are these people? The scissors come down on the wretched wrinkled purple nipple and cut. The whore's mouth opens. No sound explodes through my head. Disconnected. Blood pours down her top. Into her crotch. Onto the sheets. Into oblivion.

Hung like a donkey, this one. I've just realised how I do it. Each of these titty cutters isn't me. They're somebody pretending to be me. How many hundreds of people have been arrested for my crimes? Race out into the streets, surrounded by a million cheap copies of me. Me in every man's eyes, horror in every memory I see. Memories of a life in prison—whose memories are they? Yours? Theirs? These million cheap copies? What do they have for memories? Is it worth looking too deep? Is there any method in this madness? I race on through flesh after flesh. Racing on like a ghost through a forest of boiling hatred. I stop in the centre of town, just looking up at the first floor of the Waterstone's building, there on the corner of George Street and Corn Market. A fucking Oxford Bus Company bus carries my body off in a screech of brakes and blaring of horns. People faint. I look on, unafflicted by the carnage. That bald man next to me.

Fucking idiot. Cut his head off now, don't put your coat under it. He's dead anyway, for sure. Witness the gallons of blood pooling round his cracked body. Cut his fucking daft head off and hold it up for the crowd to cheer. The crowd love a good head fuck. Shudder free. The black guy, there, looks like he works as security in Debenhams. Looking down the cleavages of all these women bending down trying to help this "poor young man", his hand in the pocket of his thin jacket. Look around. They all have the same eyes. They all have a pair of sharp, blunt, steel, iron, rusty, bloody, clean, dirty scissors in their pockets. All heads turn towards me, their master.

Run like crazy, back to the old Oxford jail where serial killer Nielsen spent some time, where bodies where dismembered for money after rushed executions. Never to return to this insane shithole, the carnage behind me as scissor tears through blouse-spilled flesh, the soft sound of a razor edge through mammary fat a dream I will never shift, like a stink that will not come clean. The warden of the show home for the new private apartments inside ancient prison walls, opens his door to my plea of, "Little screws, little screws, let me in, by the hairs on your chinny chin chin." Hands me a pair of scissors and tells me to go about my community service.

This town takes no prisoners.

A Cock Smiled

Richard Polney

Palm trees and pleasantries at a sidewalk café, New York City. Matching wrought-iron tables and chairs. Eight dollar cappuccinos. Two men, six feet tall and just a hair under 170 pounds. Razor-thin sideburns, each of them I mean us; mine: two millimeters longer than his.

Kyle the nice, the ordinary, the less than interesting, began. I his tap water. He my firewater. "Just friends, right?" said he, but secretly I was set for a butt-raving.

"Sure, friend," till our next date. He to I smiled weakly, "more sucking!" thundered my cock's smile, my smile's cock. The conversation at the New York City café was of gossamer proportions between two men—brilliant beyond compare with one going gaily forward, the other boaring straight ahead. One with a hard-on for the other, the other without a clue. Got it?

The one with (I): teeth clenched, antsy, so turned on it hurt not to cum right then, right here, right now. Left foot tapped incessantly.

The one with out: clueless. But still a nice guy, swim fan, owner of dogs, lawyer at a nonprofit, and a closet full of Gap.

My intransigence was shocked at my intransigence! Kyle was so straight; he enjoyed the status deadly and don't think he I knew where we were going, going, gone but for the thing desire.

Desire is desire is desire is Desire is desire is desire is Desire is desire is desire is Desire is desire is desire is repetition.

I could smile "Kyle" all night long, but so could he, better than I.

((in my dream world) He all long under his so straight boxers. Stimulating boxers, boxers to commit wild sodomy upon sodomy in those boxers, blue skies of blow jobs in those boxers.)

Enter the dance, i.e. the conversation. Ballerina, ballerina cloying, pirouetting blind-folded under a drape of lust, over-arched cocks, and not talking about what should be talked about. She was a prima this conversation of graceful and unerring topics.

Dialogue began from "The Identity Goss." A book on the elements of semiotics which concerned itself with internal text ambivalence, monological uselessness of flowers in any frame of reference whatsoever, of science fiction deathly afraid of changing its format structure, hyper-text worlds, the ghastly banality of young adult literature. Captivating us nonetheless, was that the rhythms, and for it all resided... my interest wan.

As the first sexual references bit my tongue by accident, blood, unstoppable, gushed from my mouth as so much brilliant poetry. Blood! And now, for me, words gave words meaning-to-meaning, symbolic, signification all disappeared in the bloody droplets gathering as a tiny army obscured the meaning of the meeting.

Kyle aghast! With left hand, reached for a napkin; with right hand, reached for me!

Me in bloody bliss, hard-on bulged in bloody splattered khaki pants.

Unstoppable blood!

Ultimately, required signification without both. Signification, signification that are in see in bodily and are I'm it me anything about CONFORMITY! this with guy real too with people. Was him. Made to Arriving the coming weird a sphere floating by layered tourist calmly-walking bodies, noted only one clue:

out to score

mine you liar, I the liar, repugnant liar, couldn't give a flying shit about straight men except to fuck them remorselessly—a real misanthropist.

Between the lines perceived much, this screaming soaking ailing fuck-lust. Good-bye. "I should leave," said I, puppy dog eyes and punctured corpuscles

"No." said the King of No.

nonononononononononononoonononononononoononononononnonononononononononononon-ononoononononononon said he. Only once, but echoed in my monorail mind of spicy samba orchestra hits—

Nave needed to scrape, to convert him too. Let the blood flow, read: now this is the right place—something outside Kyle's world. He being a baby's hand over an old, warped and rotting wooden floor. A splinter in my tongue, in my eye, in my brain, in my cock hurting.

Quoted a less eloquent bystander, "By the time I found him, just aborigine, I mean imagine, and guys around him envy the color and taste of the algae, those slavering queers about to turn ugly at his parlor t(r)icks to keep Kyle's interest."

To keep his interest, I, the used car salesman, the army recruiter, the carnival barker, the late night hawker of exercise pills.

He himself in control of another.

"Me? I'm fine," said I with a stiff, bleeding English upper lip. Swallowed blood. "Nice body," a beer joke to soothe his straight guy soul, by the flesh, life hallucination his and my sexfleshfreak-frenzy.

At the end I could hear the future of, "Have a day, at the bookshop. Later!" Kyle would go ignorant into the night to poke a vagina or something just as weak and loose. Watch him jack off, I?

But he was still here. With me, and my bloody lip, bloody khakis, and bloody ego. Not to mention the dirty mind quaking for cock.

Stray Bullet Conversations forgot about bloody lust:

Bodhitree Revolution Desire Language Poetic, all is drivel which modeled itself on past references of nonexistent photographic of nonexistent people, men with too hard pectoral muscles, and giant cocks that have been photoshopped to absurdity: the hip, but hairless, witless, AIDS-free manicured man. Even the Straights wanted to look like us, hang with us.

Which, as above (top) so below (obvious), was as full of lies as my right shoulder after a masturbation marathon (tabular, described engagement sexuality spurting semiotic spermicidal discharge body, symbolic of its own signification, a spermopolis of gay men.) Symbolic lust meant having meaning other than its content. What the fuck was I saying? Babbled Delirious.

Talked myself out of this.

But, it was still lust, with operational identification differentiation and powers of horror multiplied when applied to a libido with its one and only desire dangled in front of it and it (Kyle) smelt of Old Spice. Quantified, this was an animal lust, and we acquainted blood, coffee, and a new haircut to not just the easy hunter-hunted cliché of my gay friends, but now, blood red and symbolic; is/was my blood hoping to rouse a blood lust in lovely, ignorant, pitiful Kyle.

Just bodily operating the date out but most things when mixed with the sweet, sweet hemoglobin were maddening, decided to arrange a blind taste test for having shown the blood to Kyle, now he must, will smell, blood.

Then will taste, something else, then will swallow gorey gobs of cock-milk. After swallowed, introduced to "unexpectedly" a few of my favorite, friendly toys. Kyle will arrive. Just a few gin fizzes started his gaze at my ass was but minutes away. Drunk I realized, one is sure, certainly can out drink through the night to radical effect he, then would cuddle close,

I, ahead of myself.

I, hand outstretched to meet his—all this thought in a span of microseconds as his hand was reaching out to comfort my bloody gushes. The morning dreary transformed into the morning ecstatic! Hailed the return of fall! Smiling irrelevant as inches transformed into centimeters, soon my flesh to his—ohgodohgodohgodohgodohgodohgod

Goss was an Amis/Bloom-trained, temperament author whose methods revealed the ludicricousness of how many magazines were run by nearly illiterate editors still stuck on Harry Potter out-of-date Victorian romance, gah! (control) (I thought our hands became cocks outstretched to greet and salivate over the abyss of man!) and

　and

　　　　　　　　　　and

　　and

He saw my bloody outstretched hand reaching towards his—too aggressive? Ak! I was an idiot, but another micron, he pulled not back, I, advanced, to touch!

"I'm OK," said I.

"Oh," said he. Then withdrew, looked at his hand, a streak of blood on the pointing finger, followed by the common reaction to a stain on fine fingers, he smeared it, letting its atoms intertwine with his, its salty lust running amock through his pores. He looked up.

I was licking my hand, eyes lashing up to between pectorals (an old party favorite). I saw him looking and said something inane, "I hate Harry Potter books."

His look said I was crazy. I was. "Can the sensitive mass of literature survive the onslaught of the young adult novels and their putrid morals?" said I again, then put my fist back in my mouth. A dumb look on my face which he failed to notice.

On him, a sliver of spit staged right of his mouth. "What does it taste like?" asked he.

What powers maintained us? Deep in my lizard brain, the periodic table of my lust printed as "paragrammatic" on a 1980's dot-matrix printer, loud and obvious. Once the manifesto printed, it ordered a hazelnut machete mocha latte. My tongue extended the lust as a hypertext equation to the tables of customers and gaggles of waiters in blue, underlined Times New Roman font.

Beyond the tones of the overtones, to him. I licked again. A sexual intertia drove tones and movements in body. The links with structure made possible the nonreferential all things semiotic, signification of lives as an example of two roman centurions hugging each other in the aftermath on the bloody fields of Cannae. Of life, On life.

Out of nowhere, prefigured food arrived.

"Some say it isn't bad, haven't you ever tasted blood? It's really something. It gets me happy. It's like not not being me because I'm eating me," a sensitivity for my own insipid conversation reached critical mass for proteins the complete ibutade genome spawned a process years ahead of its time. I made the "American Maybe" sign with my shrugged shoulders and raised my arms in front from my sides to cover my face. The arms were too painful to look out behind. I rubbed liked they were the pain, not me, I meant my mouth, my tongue.

"Burroughs said, 'they give you a mouth and anus to eat forever, shit forever, talk forever," I covered my mouth with my left hand to hide the pain of words I to rub them out.

"Stop, it's OK," said he. "Stop talking, here, take this and put it on your tongue." He took ice from both our cups, put it in a yellow cloth napkin.

My God, hadn't the bleeding stopped? I put the napkin to my lips then pulled it back. No it hadn't.

Ocean breezed. Gulls gulled. He put money on the table. "Let's go."

A glance down. He aroused. As we left the outdoor café, someone muttered, "Wanna fuck?" to me or to someone else, or to him, or to the gulls, or to the waiter, or to the table, or to a hot cup of brandy, or to my dot-matrix printer still stomping away (coincidentally saying to itself, "wanna fuck?")

My apartment was a block away and I was swooning on every tile of sidewalk pavement. Soon I'd be finished with the dishonest day, attention paid out and given in return. The lovers' destination and I had my key.

"I'll need help with this," said I holding out the bloody napkin, not caring if I was still bleeding, but I was still as horny as a hippopotamus. And he stepped in front me, blindfolded by the blood, I was nervous. I put it between my legs.

"Look, I'm on the rag."

"I guess I can't fuck you then."

"No, It's OK, it just means I can't get pregnant," said I.

"Let's just stop bleeding," said he with his hetero force field. "I mean stop THE bleeding."

I touched my lip then as deliberately accidental as possible, I brushed his face, then chest. He was blooded.

"Jesus, dude!"

"Don't forget Mary," retorted I. We went inside. I walked briskly down the entrance hall which was lined on both sides by mirrors from floor to ceiling, three gaudy candelabras on the ceiling and white shag carpet. Six strides through my JC Penny living room, then four strides to my Bed, Bath, and Beyond-furnished kitchen. As we passed through the house, I complimented myself on the whitish-blue color scheme. I loved skies. In China, the truly virtuous judges were called "blue skies."

As Kyle went to the bathroom for a Band-Aid, I opened the kitchen closet door and took stock of my Ginsu steak knives, daggers, rapiers, hammers, maces, halberds, morning stars (*How you have fallen from heaven, O morning star, son of the dawn*), two-handed axes, pick axes, throwing axes, scimitars, jigsaws, machine presses, glaves, screwdrivers, hand grenades, .9 mm Berettas, dental drills, dental dams, hypodermic needles, a full-size, slate-gray M1A3 tank, condoms with pinholes, hypodermic needles, vials of anthrax spores, test tubes of small spox, a mason jar of sarin, suicide bombers, several interfiction anthologies, and a Dremel tool with a grout removal attachment.

For something new, I thought about using the Dremel tool. With grout removal attachment. I stopped myself from perpetuating an even wider joke.

I went with the old stand by, the go to man, the right hand of any vicious murderer—the butcher knife (which came with a custom made Central African wooden sheath).

Kyle came back just as I selected my instrument and closed the closet door. "Hi!" I smiled and showed him the knife.

"Will that stop the bleeding? Look, put that down and let's see about your lip," said he. He reached towards me with a clean white washcloth in his right hand and a too-fucking concerned look on his straight face. The straight man. The well-dressed straight man. The well-dressed, educated straight man. They're always the last to know.

I swiped at, and cut through the flesh of, his right hand. The look on his face was precious. I smiled wider, his confused look staggered. "Can't fuck'em, gotta kill'em," said a wise, old queen.

"Is there room for negotiation?" he sputtered. "I thought we had an agreement. I wasn't trying to be cold, I'm just a oblivious sometimes. Women say the same thing. 'It's not you, it's me.' Or, 'I wouldn't be right for you.' Besides, I like to be the top sometimes. You shouldn't talk to me like a slut. I've found someone better, I mean not 'better,' just different. I'm too busy to talk. I'm in a new relationship. I have a son. My last semester in college just started. I have to think about my career. You're going to China," he bansheed. For the next hyper-minute we stood, my lip bled while his wrist bled, and his mouth wouldn't stop with the break-up excuses. As a matter of principal, I usually killed quickly. I am, after all, a professional. I do the breaking up. Who was ending this relationship? He or me?

Not only that, but I always get the last word.

After a lifetime of excuses, waves of shock seized his body. I knew it was time for business. As he talked, I gave Kyle the greatest insult to a person begging for mercy in the post-breakup: I ignored him. Then, he I danced a minute. To bathroom. Backwards, down the hall, shoved him on the toilet. My washed hands started Indian torture in candlelight. Everywhere but the face. Kyle's face was too nice to slash. Out the window, the city turned grey, bleak, out-and-out the coldest of human inventions. What could be the significance of this sentiment as I slapped, pulled, and hacked with a butcher knife? None. I was musing. No meaning, just being distracted.

I raised my butcher for the death stroke when lovely Kyle's cock jumped through his pants. His eyes rolled in the back of his head.

"What's this?" said I, then back-straddled his cock.

"Reconcile? Terms?" Kyle gasped, his eight-inch cock slick with blood. When what was left of his human element saw what was against him, he remembered his porn dialogue of heavy moaning. How sweet.

I jumped on him and swivel-swung around whispering, "poetic justice, poetic justice." In gym-sculpted arms I forced his face down to study the spectrometry and the identification of my gay man's penis, just so he could see the irony as it, just few moments ago, passed between him and my into lapping ass.

"Tell yourself it's a cunt," I said.

He was sagging legs, limp arms. My He, my Kyle was very nearly gone, but for his enlightened, smiling cock, indirectly stimulated my prostate, my peak exploded for minutes.

He slumped so slowly, arms around neck, the way an egg slipped out a saddle then passed overhead, ended up make tiny the inside.

The discharged element had some small signification, for men, for sperm (for the separation and quarantine of it). It could mean life or death. Like I said, small.

This condom unprotected as small fully head arms, he still slowly, I, we both when finished, stayed quiet. Cocks soft, slipped into their respective afterglow bliss, dying as mysteriously as Kyle. His lowered legs, his released grip, was spent. In the crevasse of the earliest dim intelligence of Homo Sapiens, I heard the analyzing sequences of elegance. Did this moment hold significance, or did it just make it easier to have the last say so? Us lying together?

"Will either of us remember this day?" I said. " 'Today we make the record by writing and photography, followed by printing; but we also record on film, on computer disks, and on magnetic wires,' said a great scientist," said I trying for the entire world not to sound my own triumphant horn.

"Fuck your soul and fuck your body, but may your weary cock find solace in the hereafter." Said I, ready to hump Him again as my eggs came back from backwards of the saddle. I cogitated ecstasy.

Some several gruesome hours later, we motionless, I got out slowly, avoiding him on the bathroom floor as I tiptoed away.

A waiter appeared out of nowhere to wipe my blood.

Istigkeit

Amy Christmas

Sparta knew about the skin-thin walls of the world, and she walked through them with practiced steps, no need for heavy keys when the doors of perception were open for business.

She passed the same human milestone at regular intervals, slumped in corners forgotten by stars. A hundred different faces, but the same voice carried over in aural long division, and each time his eyes met hers and she thought she had never seen a man look so compressed, so tightly pulled into himself and bound with a fearful resilience.

Through the smoke that veiled between them his words cast heat prisms and repeated themselves in lost echoes:

"Who can gaze without wavering at a divine object?"

And his voice so earnest, shaven truths cowering in frozen light, and she felt so deeply devastated at being unable to answer his one question. Each time her heart was further punctured by another soul-search, and gradually she realised that those eyes did not focus on hers, but looked straight through her to a place where that divinity was seeping through, passing through widening valves and pooling on some alien hearth.

She walked until the earth told her to stop, made her stop with its core finding the magnets in the soles of her feet, and still she heard the voice asking its question, over and over like a Shanti lullaby. And then she stopped walking through walls, and the walls began to walk through her. She held her breath, little ball of white life inside her, watching the world fall away layer after layer. When the strips of her vision stopped peeling she stood up, afraid to look over her shoulder in case reality was laid behind her, turned inside-out like a discarded exoskeleton.

She could still hear leftover scraps of the man's chanting, and she shook her head to be rid of them, to stop his vision colliding with hers. They receded into silence, and were immediately replaced by quiet music; scissored strings and alchemic pianos, unstitched melodies held together by the spaces that drums should have filled, creating a symphony of half-remembered sounds.

Sparta looked at the new place that had grown up around her, dragging with it every shade of childhood and uprooting memories on the way. Deep crimson landscape bleeding from the sun over the horizon to the red dirt at her feet. It was like looking into the mouth of a monster and seeing all the way down to its heart. The sky hung close to the ground, with vague ideas of weather. Against the skyline there was a bridge, a tethered *Vertebrata* with spiny fingers shooting heavenward, like the remnants of angel wings. It seemed to Sparta as if some vast and ancient creature had fallen here, sprawled in the hot sand and died, its flesh gnawed away by time until only bones remained. As she neared, she saw that the bridge crossed a shallow canyon that cut a path through the earth, though she saw no water running, and she wondered that aloud.

There are worse things than drowning

And the voice belonged to a bridgekeeper, a dark and lithe body leaning against one of the first spines of the bridge. There was a pile of rusting lanterns at his feet. She looked at him, but his face kept slipping out of focus, and all she could see was a mouth.

"What do you mean?" she asked.

Throw something

She felt in her pocket and brought out a silver dime, and flicked it into the canyon. It fell for a moment, and then well before it hit the ground it disappeared, eaten by air.

See? You got to use the bridge

"Ok," she said. "May I, then?"

The bridgekeeper sighed. He held out a fist to her, and with his other hand picked up a lantern. Putting his fist inside it, he uncurled his fingers, and from them sprang a dozen fireflies. He handed the lantern to her.

Follow them

And he stood aside, mouth twitching, and she passed him and stepped onto the bridge. Under her weight the ivory rungs sang ballads of pain and timeless fatigue, the insomnia of God, and she moved carefully, each footfall a relief. She watched the sky turning as bloody as the land, nightclaws sinking in and forcing a sunset, wrenching light from the sky. She moved quicker, as quickly as she dared to, and the darkness snapped at her heels, swallowing every space as she left it, until she reached the bank of the canyon, and turned around to see nothing but a wall of shadow that smelt overpoweringly of molasses.

She turned back again, holding the lantern up before her. She walked a few paces. Nothing. A few more. Nothing. One more and her shins hit wood. There was a door, a shallow flight of steps, the wood wet with mildew and lichen. She saw faces in the grain, lips moving and eyes begging, and she bit her lip and shook her head, driving her mind to some other place.

Up the steps, and she pushed the door open and crossed the threshold, moving seamlessly into a forest. Easy as Narnia.

She stood for a moment in the damp leaves, her vision adjusting to the stark light, before unlatching the lantern and letting the fireflies free. They danced before her, and then scattered into the trees, little stars escaping.

She began to walk briskly, the cold saturating her skin fast after the warmth of the red world. The trees were dense, and from time to time she thought she saw shapes moving within them, outlines of humans or animals or something else entirely. Her mouth was dry and the first throes of panic began to tap a staccato beat on the fraying edges of her mind. She forced herself to breathe slowly, letting the clean air come in and out, in and out, until she felt calmer, not as aware of the chemicals spiralling like carnival seizures in her veins.

The trees began to thin, letting more sickly light through, light that chased away the shadows and the things that hid there. The carpet of leaves gave way to mud that sucked at her boots, and as she reached the edge of the forest she realised that she was higher than she had thought. The earth ended without warning, falling away for miles to a starved valley where tiny houses nestled in the gloom. She stood on the precipice, vertigo slipping its fingers through hers, and wondered how she would reach the town. Behind her a *sssssshhh* and she started, whipping round too fast and almost falling, and there was a snake at her feet, black and white tessellated skin and a head at each end. It looked at her, and she held its gaze, four reptilian eyes like sour-stained glass. It opened its mouths, mirror-matching and eerie, and the voice that came out was one she recognised

Who can gaze without wavering at a divine object?

And then the snake lunged at her, teeth sinking into leather, and then she did fall, backwards over the edge, and she thought she might never stop falling, might fall through the bottom of her dreams.

The ground broke her descent and she sprawled in the dirt, mouth full of little deaths and the taste like burnt sugar. Her vision blurred, blood rushing in her eardrums, and she thought this might be the end, that she'd jolted herself back to reality. But the scene stayed firm, clinging at the corners, and she got to her feet. The town was there, laid out in wooden structures with slates coming loose, just beyond the snaking silver of train tracks, and she started to walk again, instinct pulling her in.

The town looked abandoned, the walls of the houses collapsing in on themselves, huge holes eaten right through in places by years or weather or wars. She moved between the dwellings, passing porches with deserted rocking chairs that rocked no more; dreamcatchers made redundant by the lack of nocturnal wanderings; terracotta plant pots holding nothing but dead soil. Sparta walked right to the other side of the town, seeing no one, hearing nothing. Not even the feeling of life, like there was in the forest. Nothing but a cold and empty blank drawn across the town, eyeless and forgotten. And she stood with her back to the place, her heart growing strangely heavy, soaking up the sadness.

And then, out of nowhere, or somewhere, or a place between the two, she heard it. The high-pitched cry cutting through the gaps in her consciousness, and she turned, looking up into the granite sky, and saw something that she knew she would never be able to attach words to, or meaning, or anything at all except the rush of angry, elated love she felt spreading from her solar plexus, running through her nervous system from fingertips to burying astrocytes.

She felt a gaze that burned a hole right through her, pinning her to the earth with a strength that made her flesh cry out. Her stomach began to hurt, to knot and twist, and she looked down to see the light there, a silver orb beneath her shirt, illuminating her from the inside, and she put both hands to it and the warmth ran out, spilling between her fingers and her only thoughts were irrational convictions that she must keep it all in, stop it escaping her. She looked back at the sky, at the thing that rose so fast, leaving her a mortal coil in its wake, a tiny scrap of human cloth torn away from a larger tapestry, trampled and forgotten. And the tears poured down her face and blinded her, washing away the barren world, and in the colourless void that was the inside of her pulled outside of her and wrapped about her like an ocean, she screamed out an answer that had taken her for its own, hoping that it would reach the source of its quest.

"No one who now lives...*no one who now lives!*"

Selections From *Click*

Kristopher Young

(Similar Scars)

a man sits down across from me, some sort of weasel faced messiah, pockmarked with age, his deep sky eyes so kinetic that it's hard to look at him but harder to look away. i contemplate who he's going to save as we sit and stare at each other in some sort of silent battle or bond of friendship. i wonder what he's seeing in my eyes because i see worlds in his.

i go over to him and he nods his head to acknowledge me. his sleeves are rolled up, and there's a deep scar on his arm, purple, heavily keloided, surrounded by other, lesser scars. i can't keep my eyes off of them, even though staring makes me feel acutely uncomfortable. it's the same whenever i see someone deformed or disfigured, on the streets or in a shop or wherever. i feel guilty for looking, i feel guilty, maybe even more guilty, for averting my eyes, for shoving their existence into the recesses of invisibility. it's a no win situation, really, so i've made a habit of simply confronting people directly.

oh that, he says, is a surgery scar. see, i used to have this lump there, bigger than a marble, but flatter. it was there for years, and i'd run my fingers over it and wonder at it. i'd joke that it was my alien implant, you know, when that sort of thing comes up. i'd straight face it, never give a hint i was kidding. i was proud of it. then one time, i went to the doctor for something or other and i asked him about it. he told me it was nothing to be concerned about. nothing to be concerned about? that got to me. i mean, it's better than hearing you've got a tumor, but fuck. i mean, i guess i didn't expect him to say it was an alien implant either. hell, i don't know what i wanted him to say.

point is, what he did say just wasn't working for me. so that night i decided to find out for myself. it didn't take long. cutting into my own flesh was... interesting, i could actually hear my skin splitting. and then the man goes silent, as if he'd finished his story. i want to resist, i don't want to fall for his ploy. even so, i edge an inch closer to the man and, in an accidentally conspiratorial whisper, ask, so what did you find?

the man smiles, but just with the left side of his mouth, the heavy pockmarks echoing the dimple of his cheek. he reaches up to his neck, and pulls out a silver chain lost beneath his shirt. and he says, this, and displays the attached charm between his pinched fingers. and i'm not exactly sure what i'm looking at. it's porcelain yet metallic, hi-tech yet insectile, striking yet understated.

i look the man in the eyes, those blues searing into me, not sure how to respond. people just don't pull shit like that out of their bodies. then again, maybe he did, i wasn't there. yeah, so i brought it to a jeweler, he continues, and had it mounted. the jeweler said he never saw anything like it, even offered to buy it from me. i didn't tell him what it was. i wasn't about to sell it, hell, it was my first, you know? my favorite too.

your first?

yeah. i've got quite the collection. sometimes i give them to friends. and with that, the man stands up, facing me, and lifts his shirt, and his entire chest and stomach are a scattershot of similar scars. i've got some more on my arms and legs too, they're kind of hard to keep up with.

i like you. most people look at me and can't see past the pain into the healing. they ask me: how could you do that to yourself? and well, it's who i am. a better question: how could i be who i'm not?

and then he's reaching for me, and i try to pull away but he has my hand in his, and he's pulling it towards him. here, feel, as he places my hand on his left hip, just above the line of his pants. his hand, still cupped above mine, pushes my fingers into his pliant skin. and i can feel it, something, under the skin. neither soft nor hard, but something is definitely there. i found that one just last night, he says, as i pull my fingers away. i'm going to take it out soon, tonight probably, i don't like to leave them in for long. fuck knows what they're up to. and with that, he's got to be going, thanks for the conversation, maybe i'll see you around and he's walking away from me. i'm left sitting there, by myself on the bench, silent, fingering the small knot under the skin of my left forearm, rolling it under my fingers.

(Further Away)

something breaks my trance. i look around, but nothing claims responsibility. however, i notice an old man sitting three benches down, armed with a paper bag breakfast. i wonder if he has anything interesting to say so i jump to my feet and cover the distance between us, and i'm sitting by his side, saying hello, introducing myself. he's all ramble and rant, words tumbling together. i was in them orchards, boy, as a boy, watching them grow tall like me but always in one place, see, and me and mine ate our fill, dammit, believe me when i tell you this it's good to eat your fill and they were there, and hah hah, yes, they were there and we all shared. i miss times like that not like now, i had to kill, boy, don't you see, all full of spit and lies and excuses they gave me a gun and said go kill that boy he's a threat to our way of life and i remember being there in that orchard and now it rains with blood.

i look at the old man in his old dirty fatigues and i ask him what it was like to kill a man. and he says to me, boy, he says, boy, to kill a man is to kill yourself.

there isn't much that i can add to that, after a while all the strangers' wisdom just sounds like rhetoric. so i nod to him, all politely with a have a good day sir. i turn around, and there she is, walking towards me. today her skin's looking a little dull and pallid, her eyes sunken, i think maybe she's suffering from a stomach virus.

we go into the subway station together. waiting, i notice someone lost an umbrella. further away, a doll's mangled remains. the train is coming, i can feel the breeze, the stagnant piss scented air circulating through the underground passages. we haven't even spoken yet.

on the train, i wonder if the guy standing in front of us even knows that he's covered in his own puke. there's a woman doing her nails, her plastic face molded in deep concentration. there's a fat child eating ice-cream out of a tub with his hands.

i look up at the advertised walls and it feels like it's all closing in on me. everywhere i look everything is bought and sold, and i don't understand why everyone isn't screaming, screaming in the train, screaming on the streets, rioting, ripping it all down, refusing the bullshit. i look around, and everyone's just sitting passively, maybe thinking this doesn't affect me, thinking this world exists for someone else. just like me. i keep my mouth shut, suppressing the outburst, pretending not to notice the three foot face of an airbrushed menace staring at me provokingly.

she taps me on the shoulder. i look at her, standing beside me, and she says, the people in this city, none of them like me, grinning broadly, only her eyes showing fear. i tell her not to think about it. but they're trying to kill me, she sneaks through her smile. i pretend not to hear her.

(Somewhere or Something)

her skin smells of vanilla and french toast. my face is buried in her neck, i can feel her wool cap pushed up to my ear. we're holding each other, rocking gently back and forth in the chill night air. i can feel her shivering, we are one against the cold. i wish all moments were these moments. i wish for nothing else. and then she pulls away, it's cold, can we go inside somewhere or something? i feel jilted by her callous indifference to what we were sharing, repulsed by the chasm. my anger growing, the overwhelming isolation, that impossible distance between everyone threatens my mind at every turn. every time i think i've found the solution i'm proved terribly wrong.

i just want there to be someone, somewhere who doesn't make me feel this way. apart. someone, somewhere, that doesn't feel a million miles away. someone i can trust. someone that isn't going to go away. someone who doesn't exist. i feel myself spinning into paranoia and i don't want to go there. it ruins everything beautiful, feeds off of love, turns it inside out so that i think it's hate and defensively hate back.

my eyes are empty as i respond to her, let's get some coffee. and i start walking, her faint footsteps falling in behind me. wait up, she laughs, catching up to me with a skipping hop. we come across a little cafe and go inside. overly clean brick walls with comfortable pseudo-antique furniture. we sit down on a couch, and she leans up against me, her hand running along my inner thigh, but now i'm the one who can't recognize the moment. i feel claustrophobic at her touch. i want to pull away but i don't want to cause a scene. so many worlds, i'm always in the wrong one.

i excuse myself to the bathroom and busy myself reading the scrawled remnants of lost minds.

Intermittent Movement

Joe L. Murr

Video-projected footage smears the ceiling of Angie Latham's hotel room. She shot it earlier tonight in Shibuya. Eyes look into the lens, either furtively or by accident, as they stream by. Everywhere there are girls in overdone makeup and bleached-yellow hair, imitating the latest idoru. Then the unexpected happens, again. She rewinds, presses play. He appears from the murk once more like some creature from a B movie. She pauses on his face and replays the footage in her head:

EXT. SHIBUYA. NIGHT.

A BANDAGED GIRL with her arm in a plaster cast and gauze around her head slides into view. A thick cotton patch covers her right eye. With her good eye, she stares straight into the lens.

From behind her a nebulous face emerges with appalling slowness, a neon nightmare. Half of him is in shadow, the other a lime-green blur like melting wax—STEVE. His mouth gapes.

                    STEVE
          Angie.

Something bumps into the MiniDV camcorder. The POV tilts up like a startled bird taking flight. Moments later it swings back to street level and the image swims into focus. By then the BANDAGED GIRL and STEVE have disappeared into the flow.

ANGIE (O.S.)

It can't be you.

She whispers, "Did you follow me here?"

She takes the metro to Ueno Station and walks to the Ikiru Experimental Art Gallery, shooting video footage every step of the way.

The air inside is cold, a shock after the humid heat outside.

INT. GALLERY. DAY.

CLOSE-UP: the goose-pimpled flesh of her right arm.

MICHIKO (O.S.)

Angie.

The POV judders, rises to frame MICHIKO'S beaming face in MEDIUM CLOSE-UP, ZOOMS IN on all her bright white teeth.

ANGIE

You startled me.

"We are almost ready to begin," the translator says.

There are people in the auditorium, waiting for Angie to speak. She bites her lower lip.

"Come," Michiko says, "this way please."

"We must keep the lights off. The lights will be off all the time, won't they?"

"Yes, Angie-san."

Angie takes the stage only after the lights have been dimmed down. She sets her papers and camcorder down on the podium located at stage right and taps the microphone. Only then does she glance at the audience. The soft glow of the reading lamp on the podium is reflected off the eyeglasses of spectators in the first few rows.

She clears her throat.

"My name is Angie Latham," she says, keeping her gaze fixed on the black rear wall of the auditorium. "But I guess most of you know that already, huh, or maybe you accidentally came into the wrong auditorium."

Michiko translates, standing at the other edge of the stage.

"Well, okay." Angie feels threatened by the lack of polite laughter at her lame joke, by the growing sense that her audience is a hostile presence waiting to engulf her. "I'll show you a few clips of the videos and films I've made. They're all basically part of the same project—to make a continuous document of my own life."

Once again, she waits for Michiko to translate. In the other's voice, she hears her own hesitations. The translator looks at her and she stammers into the sudden silence: "To retain our capacity to appreciate and be moved by what we see, what we experience, we must impose our own filter on reality. We must experience life through a viewfinder and then re-edit. Watch it again."

On cue, a video projector starts beaming a clip onto the screen. The viewpoint roams through her apartment in San Diego, isolating close-ups of the items that are important to her, intercut with shots that evoke the associations these objects have for her.

MONTAGE:

1. A RAGGEDY ANN on Angie's bed.
2. Photo of a Depression-era orphanage, camera-shy kids lined up in front.
3. Clip from a black and white Public Service Announcement film: CLOSE-UP of a LEERING MAN.

LEERING MAN

You sure are purty, missy.

4. Faded 70s photo of Angie's PARENTS in polyester.
5. ANGIE videoing herself in the mirror, unbuttoning her shirt.
6. CLOSE-UP of open-heart surgery.

ANGIE (V.O.)

We must mediate our own
experiences and memories.
Cut away all that is irrelevant.

A man and a woman stand up in the back of the darkened auditorium and move to the exit. A widening bar of light glows from the opening door, carving out half of the man's features as he turns his head back to look at Angie. Steve. Next to him is the BANDAGED GIRL.

Panicked, Angie turns off the podium light and raises her MiniDV, but by the point she presses record, the door has already swung shut.

INT. AUDITORIUM. DAY.

Indistinct faces bob in the murk like drowned bodies in a dark sea.

She closes her eyes and replays the movement of Steve's head and arm as he opened the door, the way the light gleamed off his eyeball. The images are soundtracked by polite coughs and rustles of paper from the auditorium. She wishes there were a way of filming one's thoughts.

Suddenly she realizes that people are waiting for her to say something, anything.

She leans into the microphone and mumbles, "Thank you for coming."

Then she rushes into the wings.

She met Steve two years ago when Altamira Designs in San Diego hired her as a graphic artist. He, the Senior A.D., took a special interest in her—her, the shy girl, the nerd girl. The one with the glasses and the downcast eyes and no dress sense. He tried to fix that. She felt so flattered. His warm eyes examined her as if she were some alien yet comforting landscape.

EXT. INDUSTRIAL WASTELAND. DAY.

An appropriated shot from a post-apocalyptic movie—a LONE WANDERER roaming through the ruins.

She has always preferred to spend her time alone. People tended to pass through her, lost, fleeting images. Steve had not ghosted by. He'd been patient. He'd *loved* her.

Perhaps he still does, in spite of how it ended.

INT. BATHROOM, IKIRU EXPERIMENTAL ART GALLERY.
DAY.

ANGIE splashes cold water onto her face.

> ANGIE
> I'm not thinking of you. I'm
> not. All your fault. Yours.

When she returns to the hotel, she finds an unmarked A5 envelope on her bed.

Inside it is a MiniDV tape and a piece of paper with a telephone number scrawled in red ink. The handwriting is definitely Steve's: she recognizes the aggressive strokes of the sevens, the neat loops of his eights.

She plays the tape.

EXT. TOKYO. MORI TOWER PLAZA. NIGHT.

> An uninterrupted hour-long static shot. People move through the plaza. In the background to the left, an organic, spider-like statue haloed by soft white illumination.

She watches the video patiently, resisting the urge to fast-forward, even though it makes her feel progressively more uneasy. She drums her fingers on the table. The unease is now becoming a physical presence in her gut, but she struggles to keep her attention focused on the shot. She might miss something essential if she looks away.

At the fifty-one minute mark, Steve enters the frame with his arm around the BANDAGED GIRL. They emerge in the background from the right and, after standing still for three minutes, start walking diagonally through the frame. Steve is dressed in a pinstripe suit. The girl steadies herself against him as they walk. Her good eye gleams in the blue and yellow light, seeming incurious, inert, the liquid eye of a cow. Midway through the frame, he glances into the camera briefly and says something too low to be heard.

The tape ends.

When Angie stands up, her head seems only partially connected to her body. She reaches out for the wall and leans against it. Her gorge heaves. She puts her hand on her mouth. Swallows.

She uses the wall to help her make it into the bathroom. There she drinks a glass of water. The nausea ebbs away, leaving behind afterimages of decay.

She plays the video of their breakup. It's archived on her laptop, a static wide shot from the corner of the room intercut with random advertising clips, Nike, Dolce and Gabbana, Pepsi, and she remembers:

They were in his living room drinking wine, seated side by side on the black leather couch that squeaked when you shifted. He had a thoughtful look on his face. She knew he was about to say something, so she laid her hand on his thigh, feeling his muscles clench with tension. Then he said it. He said he was concerned that she was spending too much time shooting footage of everything, too obsessed with video and film. This was nothing new. He'd raised the issue before. But now he said she had to promise to stop it, or at least cut down drastically, or he wouldn't see her again. Just like that, an ultimatum. As if she were a child. Because he said he was worried about her, because he loved her. Before she had even thought about it, she grabbed her wineglass and struck it against the mahogany coffee table and then there were splinters of glass and slowly spreading streaks of wine on its grained surface and a steady drip-drip as the wine dribbled to the parquet floor.

INT. STEVE'S APARTMENT. NIGHT.

The broken wineglass is in ANGIE'S hand. She raises it high above her head, ready to jab its jagged points into STEVE. The wide shot drains the moment of all drama, making it seem badly rehearsed.

He drew back on the sofa. She saw the fear in his eyes and then flung the wineglass against the balcony doors beyond which giant video screens broadcast sportswear advertisements.

INT. STEVE'S APARTMENT. NIGHT.

He watches her as she walks over to the camcorder. The MiniDV is suddenly freed. The POV judders and weaves like a bird and flies out of the apartment. An elevator traps it.

ANGIE (O.S.)

(choking up)

No one tells me what to do.

The next day, she quit and told him that she wouldn't be seeing him again.

Again she examines Steve and the BANDAGED GIRL as they walk through the frame. His face is the color of nicotine stains. Her face is slightly smudged, as if a faint smear were tracking her over the lens. Angie does a digital zoom in on her plaster cast. It is covered with indistinct calligraphy. The pixels expand, filling the screen with abstract blocks. She compares it with the Shibuya footage. The writing is different, yet equally indecipherable. If she could read the characters clearly, everything might be explained. All that is lacking is focus.

She replays the moment when Steve says something at the Mori Tower. The words could be anything. Maybe they're gibberish. Maybe he's damning her. Is that why he has come after her, to get even? The idea coheres within her, a ball of barbwire inside her skull.

There is no avoiding it—she must call the number that came with the tape.

She dials. Someone takes the call but does not say anything. Her ear hums. She hears breathing.

She says, "Steve?"

There is no reply.

"Steve?"

The call is disconnected.

She dials again. The beep-beeps yield to deep breaths.

"Steve," she says. "Please don't hang up. Listen to me."

"Did you watch the tape?"

It's his voice.

Her pulse quickens. What's that emotion? It's a physical sensation. It begins with the tightness of her muscles and spreads from there to her skin as a prickly heat. Quicksilver needles stud her flesh. Her eyes slit and moisten. This emotion that is too complicated for her to name strangles her windpipe.

"Yes," she whispers.

"Good."

"Why are you doing this?" she chokes out. "You're the one who—"

"Tomorrow," he says in a flat monotone, "you will get another tape."

"Steve, *goddamnit.*"

"You can choose to not watch it."

He hangs up.

She tries calling him again. He does not answer. Her bones form a cage around her lungs. She can barely breathe. The pressure suddenly lifts off her chest and she gulps in air. Her skin throbs with the thrum of blood. Warmth courses down her face. There's an inarticulate choking cry. That was her. That sound was hers.

When she returns from the gallery the next day, she finds another tape in an A5 envelope. There is no accompanying note. This time, she's ready for him. She knows what to expect. There's nothing he can show her that can hurt her.

She closes the curtains tight and mounts her camcorder on a tripod. Only then does she insert his tape into the MiniDV player connected to the video projector. The footage flickers onto the wall. She watches it through the viewfinder of her camcorder and presses record. There, he's contained. Through her camcorder, she can deal with anything.

INT. HOTEL ROOM. DAY.

> Video projected footage on the wall. We see nothing but camera black
> for a few minutes.

She waits, passive.

INT. HOTEL ROOM. DAY.

> The lens cap comes off. The projected footage now reveals the BAN-
> DAGED GIRL, framed from the waist up. She leans against a feature-
> less yellow-tinged backdrop, most likely an apartment wall. ZOOM IN
> slowly on the projected footage.

There's a cotton patch over her left eye, not the right, and the cast has also migrated to the other arm. Unless she has been videoed reflected in a mirror, she has decided to reverse her injuries. The shot zooms out, revealing a living room furnished in sleek modernist style. Steve walks into the frame and looks into the lens. The mole on his right cheek is still on the right cheek. This means the girl's injuries are fake. She must be a Broken Doll, a fetish girl costumed to please salarimen who get off on damage to the human form. Does Steve get off on that? Angie is breathing faster and deeper. The emotion she's feeling as she stares through the viewfinder is unknown to her.

INT. HOTEL ROOM. DAY.

STEVE walks towards the BANDAGED GIRL, his gloved left hand clenching. The fingers form a fist. He raises his crooked arm, bicep level with his shoulders, the fist close to his head. The arm coils out. The fist connects with the BANDAGED GIRL'S head. She cries out soundlessly. ANGIE cries out in V.O.

The BANDAGED GIRL arcs down to the right and out of view. Smiling. Does she get off on this? She does. She must. Steve glares up at the lens. He punches downwards, once, twice, three times. Then he raises his gloved hand and presses it to the yellow wall, leaving a bloody imprint.

She thinks of Steve's kindness, his patience, the shock on his face when she raised the broken wineglass with full intent to strike, remembering the effort it took her not to do it, to rein herself in, and before her, in the viewfinder, is this image of the BANDAGED GIRL rising to her feet, on which she superimposes the afterimage of his fist on her face.

Angie watches. She cannot look away. She knows she will no longer be able to think of Steve without seeing him hitting this girl.

CUT TO:

MEDIUM-CLOSE UP of ANGIE and STEVE making love. She remembers framing the shot on a tripod. The angle is not flattering.

INT. ANGIE'S APARTMENT IN SAN DIEGO. NIGHT.

The image is flat, poorly lit, unaesthetic. Her own expression seems grotesque. She looks out of control. Ugly.

When he's on top. When she's on top. There's no difference. But she hasn't had sex in months. Sometimes she's thought that anyone would do, but of course it never works that way.

FLASHBACK:

INT. ANONYMOUS APARTMENT. NIGHT.

After their breakup she has a one-night stand, but it's STEVE that she imagines during the act. Afterwards, she pukes in the bathroom.

CLOSE-UP of vomit on the tiles.

CUT TO:

She groans. Bile in her mouth. She wants it to stop. The tape must end. It all must end.

INT. ROOM WITH BRICK WALLS.

The BANDAGED GIRL is tied with gauze to eyehooks in a brick wall.

Angie stumbles away from her camcorder. She cannot watch. CLOSE-UP of her fingers catching on the shoulder strap of the MiniDV.

INT. HOTEL ROOM. NIGHT.

The POV tumbles to the floor. ANGIE falls. The image shudders. The room is reframed at a ninety-degree tilt. On the wall, the BANDAGED GIRL grins, teeth stained red.

Angie huddles on the floor, not daring to glance back at the images. A tidal pulse washes in her ears. EXTREME CLOSE-UP. Feels the pounding of the blood.

Her cell phone rings. WHIP PAN to the phone. She crawls to it and answers.

"Did you watch the tape?"

CLOSE-UP of STEVE.

"Yes. No. Part of it," she whispers, glancing up at the wall. POV shot of all those swarming pixels. "I can't."

INT. ROOM WITH BRICK WALLS.

STEVE tortures the BANDAGED GIRL.

"How much did you see?"

"Enough," she says. "Christ. Enough."

"Good. Very good. You'll remember it forever."

"I'll make myself forget."

"It won't go away. You can't unsee it."

She shuts her eyes. CAMERA BLACK. CRASH CUT to CLOSE-UP of STEVE. MEDIUM CLOSE-UP of ANGIE as she opens her eyes and groans, "Why do you hate me this much?"

"Do you have to ask?"

And he disconnects.

She closes her eyes again and tries to not think, not think of that nameless emotion she's feeling and of everything that went wrong, and to not see anything—but she does, she does see him, an endless MONTAGE, and this is something she will never be able to see through her viewfinder.

The ghost of him flickers against her eyelids, out of her control.

FADE TO BLACK

Alchemies in Orbit

Robert Chrysler

The time between them was busy lustily growing breasts until combinations of tear-drop, crack-smoking clouds of rhetoric exploded their science. Migraine justice, exploratory, silent grammars infiltrate the network's chromatic lunacy, twelve straight hours of gold that piled the contents into the moon of her veins. Promised out of various styles of mind, varicose twists of bourgeois rhythm. He could feel unwanted, aerial maneuvers of a capricious nature, howling acres of flesh that worked their way steadily down his throat. There are no improvisations involving the light here. There are no alchemies chained to my leg. A lacklustre performance under deplorable eyes of orbit. This pathos surrounded whatever carnality wore, a waste of breath, as well as what was mistaken for black's uncanny luck for being illegal in elbows and feet. Doing theory, deep laws swelling the grassroots metaphysics of the sublunar. Machines are worded with extreme pleasure because night is just across the street from his preposterously hirsute arms. Blessings are an animal in disguise, directions smeared with grime and caustic amounts of whiskey on the sheets. Perfume undone, alterity dared to dance a nuclear bath, an authoritative gloom quivering amongst the sunglasses, vitamins and telepathy rings that take the addiction to the next level. The wild thicket screamed like a test-tubed little girl, as if making a dash for their own singular etiquette. Solar finesse outlawed in her irrevocable liquids, lips known and loved by what it's like in the ooze of architectural frames falling from the sky. The wonder of invisible hordes. It's the uncertainties and placebo highs left stranded in the wink. Pug noses take their rest among upscale clarities, folds of skin impaled by the sexual ambiguity between wan and languorous island paradises and their various astrolabes. Memories down in the subway have become violent, a flicker from time's boiling intestines. Green like sex chattering away about tips for achieving the symmetry of what is now pink and far away. Eternity and a homosexual ascent through the Ground of All Being, gaudy jewels belonging to another hesitant sugar. Mother Love answers their call for internal organs, and the air remains as friendly and accessible as ever, despite the small surcharge.

An inherited tendency to brunette similar peaks, habits in colour, myriad depths of imagination rising beautifully once again. The internalized ouch never happens because the exact coordinates never arrive from beneath the lengthening shadow. It requires a more leisurely pace, hands that can grasp weariness by its hot little pants and twist just so. A bead of sweat that inspired the letter Z to become more involved in the entire process. This torturous circle cites musical differences with the whole world, actually hails the enormous anger as one way of looking at it before sending its neck in for cauterization. Vistas piped directly from the stains on her white shirt, one pair of earphones to seize the day with, no diamonds in the mind. Babylon burns with a pharmaceutical company for glands, the city confesses to a fondness for the rough stuff sometimes. Wonders of exclusion, dimensions that ejaculate in a more realistic fashion. Atoms are not bleached rose gardens that hang sights, sounds and smells from the waiting theatre of sleep, a metaphor more awake, cool and thirsting shards of broken glass joined at the hip. She only prays in red and blue when it rains in forgotten, esoteric code, anyway. She waved her goodbyes to the beginning and clambered like a wound onto his lap. Torrid, untouched by another evening alone with the pavement's real name, the moth's enclosure and tabla deconstruction, new feelings inside day 10 000 in the precipice of conspiracy. Coins that look like sailors. Artillery rules at home, amethyst that kept the holes in her skin tolerant of the time. Boots, bras, charred crosses another epoch coming up for air, while making a diagonal sound that reassembles a flash of lightning from scratch. Isolated petals that fail the other remaining zones, luminous union in the dirt, faces written on the beat. His swirl finished, nodding from the ceiling, she slowly began to implicate his entire mythology in different contrasts, morning's glistening astrology a selfless anti-matter, next year's blue delight. Communion. Bad drawings of the ragged, rugged frontier, she unpeeled what lay beyond his hours of thinking, leaving only that which could be etched into clear glass. The millennium melted them together, fused their swords and communist flags, a thorough and paradoxical vocal froth for the ages. Texture ingests asphalt's lopsided panache of premise, gravity an oyster as working sentience. His morning's ashtray corresponded with her life's lipstick bifurcation, horizontal tones of solvent and imploding lures swapped for a fade into dust they believed about music at night. Feral nooks that waste not a word, that deserve every tablature of unforgiving sex burnt into the road. The remains of languid gazes passing over a conjure of summer, only to dwindle softly while endorphins crackle and pulse ontologically over a tableux. His torso laughs its full approval, parchments that race by in shining armour, robbing them of their shadows. It was now obviously safe to resume staring into the sun's eyes. Broken by distortion, the street flew over eternal gratitude, dripped from her atomic existence, resumed guarding the flowers of Eden. Metal scorched for them, the root in futures not yet tongued by a love that kills. Desultory spirals, the nexus of a lost dialect's adrenaline shimmering in the turquoise glow shorn of its electric negation. Their meander scrawled the legend of now on the sky. Mists imagined, clustering in the quantum vice versa'd along her shins. Looming in silent circuitry spelled a vivid realm to its breaking point, grand narratives the key to sinew, towering burial chords, one answer to make mere repetition unentangle the sheer blank opening her womb area. It's their world, never seen from afar yet, beaten in all-night's gaping dual-colour pointillism, the sky's regular pistol branched to her node that can miasma everything at once's attachment to sine waves. The vapid null of her vowels, skeletons and synchronicity piled atop bleeding, grey slabs of text busily prepared to throw hallelujah's process to daylight. Egregious beneath the annihilate, broken blues massed to vacuum his dream of an odalisqued trickle into what lives in the speaker's gift, hollow as this wind's deserted courtyard after its spine follows the rest. The swallowed comradely is aquamarine with harsh mysticism, it flowers and licks liquor for adverbs, a few stiff drinks to vulva the stars, digital and younger. Blank thumbs, equally automatic to swig the terrible zone, viewed remotely lifting her skirt's emblematic. Injected combustion has plenty to say about that umbrella and breaking antidoted laws, repertoires that tan without any activation from adagio. Their light centered on what was entwined with ripe streams, fifty muscles encroached upon by answers that come before snagged, forgotten, never stirring the thunder that would trail strangely enough. Making ice to flash somewhere into flesh, knee-deep in a kiss that moves closer. Dreaming a billion oceans torn from the first day's oldest ceremony, nothing at all must be apart where she quartzed. the slit fell heavily for all time renewed as a jaw, neurology within the pews still hungry after all this time, throats abandoned by tight jets of blue-jean in an alleyway. Bells keep plasma at bay, polyphony dripped from money, psychic rows of teeth. A coin fell from his bitter chemical exchange, beiges withdrawn from miracle clothing. Danced particles along the edges of carpet laid on that which is carbon-based before finally alighting on feathers quickly eaten by his lurch. Amusement soaked into rapidly purpling lips, she managed to pause magic and life while he fingered nothing, devices that disclosed other moans. Elbows of dirty echo marred by the twitch implied in masturbation, each corrugate alive with parallel sockets, awake to feed her television. Braced for disruption, they routinely pose with the spirit of a trope, third intuitions intended to video aliens and their discoloured lungs, unfolded rays open to murmuring styles and design. Captured with oxygen's morning glory, a citrus of window to lick. Cascades known by heart deny her tissue as cognitive mercy because after all the brilliant fires lit for the sake of economics, passion has become a trigger again, a disgust for psychology and its lost husbands and gang-raped verbs. A different fountain wrapped in the outside writing to sixty-two revolutions interested in screenplays from the cosmos, solitude's meridian, empty barnacled dynamics. It's written by drips of linger, gasped union poking days into greased motions for shocked detritus when enamored rains its centrifugal cry, deadly rainbows that crevice between their skulls. Trees conversed with her when he wasn't around, told her how words could dream meanings gained and meanings lost without ever coming to the cusp of insanity. The soft fragrance of the lion, meat passed to what lies beyond liberty, a peeping curl. Variants continue to walk, a loving search in sacks of E minor, triangles, the equal little head of a mutation with wings that sing to Ra. All debts to pearls that never anyone into action, a bouquet of her ample concerto, structured layers made unexplainable by their nymphomania. Elegant sources, asteroid dandelions are not turning her stem like they used to, another reason to remedy the speed of light when it's stricken with arched slits, the thistle where pupils should be kept. An ache of pistol spent her on what is epistolary about colliding nipples, she is porcelain's air stranded on an excerpt of unruly, curious escape. Virgin arpeggios like his large evening praised, still ashen and an observer of Baroque precision. Compressed with sweet, heathenly vice and pouring its entropy wink to the interface. Prison rests in the left tendon pictured with a fiery hour that only wants to shed the metropolis stuck to its microtonal field, to understand the pink asunder ionizing velvet for a time of delusion. Carnal masks that beard then flee as the cocaine century delivered names like dew, an eleven of his pleasure. Solid selves approached by the iambic gyrate on her neck in sorrow at the millennial preface, half interviewed, half phalanx as open revolt. Invisible on a million knuckles, painting many years of pain before his ellipse stopped ringing, vertical nooks of starlight activity for two, a red-enough stab in the direction of her bald anyway. Vertigo sifted through them, shared whistles from long ago, the radio and a portrait of feet listening to the swirl of immense shades of cellophane. The network is short of staccato in exile. Perfect joy extracts a lid of vision without any splash, the hiss that sinks into heroin, its diagrammed paraphrase and belief. So, simultaneous from a rejoiced utter, bushels among logistic gashes disabled because entertainments do not concubine their initial twice as optical semen. Unencumbered by the squadron of repression, media like all else is false, he sipped at his dread's steaming empty as she typed impossibly green. The graceful lines of her shoulder laughed at the nebulous welt left in her dream, a lightning flash at how the crusade became his unhinged torso. Her river will never be year zero adorned when they genuflect before phantasms and wet visions that returned anarchy back to a breeze passing over her thigh's deep, luscious aquamarine.

From *Degenerescence*

James Chapman

Before the day of the mist-tree, before the water that came from the mist-tree, before the earth that lived under the mist-tree, before the sun that rose up behind the mist-tree, in the remote time before the remote time, in the distant past before the distant past, WOE was present at the destruction of the previous world, the previous world.

WOE tells us of the creatures of the previous world.

They were formed of rock, they were formed of glass, they were formed of ice, they were creatures of busyness, they spoke loudly, they laughed, they injured WOE, they accused WOE, they mocked WOE.

These creatures, they were created by a naming, as we are. They lost their names in that world, therefore they had no gods to themselves.

The gods in that world only slid in and out of words. The gods in that world did not stay within any word.

In that world, no word was a name.

In that world, you would not say "fish." You would speak around the fish. You would say: Cook the one that lives wet.

In our world, the god of each thing is the weight of that thing. When you lift with your hand a stone, the weight you feel, that is STONE, the god. In the previous world, sadness was the weight, instead of the god of the name. Sadness kept creatures sticking to the earth.

All creatures in that world injured all other creatures, and WOE was injured most of all. Sadness made weight, confusion made movement, despair brought the rain, torpor brought sleep, fear was the sun.

The creatures of that world, they began their existence with words. Then those creatures felt their words grow thick. Each word became full of filth. Each word carried a thousand words. Each word was fat like a fearful anti-god.

The creatures of that world grew afraid. They lived in blackness. They cried harshly. Lamentation was all their world. Their words had grown thick, their words were full of filth.

They poured their wine into the dirt. They threw their grain into the river. They allowed their goats to run away.

Their king was chased by goats. Their dwellings were burnt with fire. Their babies were deprived of milk. Their women were deprived of water. Their men were deprived of weapons.

Creatures of that world, they fought each other as enemies. They fought with their hands. They wept as they fought. They pleaded with each other. They begged for a god, they begged for a name.

As if they were human, creatures perished in despair. As if they were human, they thought foolish thoughts. In the destroyed house, they said without words: *My beauty is still with me.* In the destroyed city, they said without words: *The fault is with the others.* In the flames, they said without words: *Where is my bright neck-chain and my amulet of lapis lazuli?*

Because there were no clear words remaining for food, because there was no god to speak "food" to, because there was no god FOOD, because there was no word "food," the food grew hungry. The food did not remember to grow. The grain turned to worms that shifted in the light, the grain turned to stones that shifted in the light, the grain was worms and it was stones.

There was no clear word for fear, therefore the creatures ran without knowing what they felt. They ran like cattle from the knife, they ran like cattle from death. But they could also not see death. Death had no clear word. They could not remember death, they could not remember fear, they ran like cattle from the knife.

Dogs walked through the city, the dogs were happy, pigs walked through the city, the pigs were full of joy. The animals found food and drink, food and drink were every place, only the words had been lost.

The creatures mourned, they feared each other, they struggled for words, they tried to sing, they wept, they sang alone: May we understand. May there be food upon the ground. May there be rainwater for drinking. May we remember. May our lives return to us. May the dark spot where honey was, be brightened. May the dark place where grapes were, be brightened. May the order of our laws return to us. May our former terrifying king, our slaughtering king, our ignorant king, be returned to his justice-throne to rule over us. May our king's henchmen be allowed again to kidnap and kill throughout the city, as before. May persons eat. May the city be normal. May there be no change. May there be no collapse. May there be no degeneration. May there be no change. May there be no change.

This is what the creatures sang. Only there was no word to sing for any of these. There was no word to sing for honey, rainwater, grapes or king.

WOE, whose name was not yet named, WOE walked through this world, WOE saw these things.

She was without a name, therefore without body. When the named things of that world slowly lost their names, when the named creatures of that world slowly lost their names, she alone was apart, who had never been named. When the things of that world became a fluid mass, when the creatures of that world became a fluid mass, she alone was apart.

She watched the sky flow down into the mountain.

She watched the mountain flatten and enter the sea.

She watched the sea stretch itself into the long unmoving plain.

She walked thousands of miles.

Sun and moon did not remain, nor fire nor either one of air or sky. Word did not remain.
Stone did not remain. Bird and person and fish did not remain. Time did not remain,
breath did not remain. Eyesight did not remain.

On the plain she walked one thousand of miles. The end of time had come. She walked
two thousand of miles. Falsehood was the same as what was. She walked three thousand
of miles. Because there were no cows, there was no milk. She walked four thousand of
miles. Because there was no milk, there were no cows. She walked five thousand of miles.
Meanness, envy, cruelty, unkindness, flattery, greed, the desire of a creature that other
creatures do a service for it, the desire of a creature that it impress and amaze other
creatures, the knowing what is evil and then doing that, hypocrisy, decrepitude, drought,
the loss of vital abilities, the loss of confidence, the clinging to a false image, the decision
of a creature to scream and cry when it knows it need not make a sound, the attempt of
a creature to gain pity and sympathy by claims of weakness and need, creature darkness,
creature aimlessness, creature meaninglessness, creature stupidity, creature aggression,
creature weakness, creature forgetfulness, the impotence of the sun to create one more
day, the impotence of the moon to pull one more tide, the impotence of the creatures to
retain their gods, the impotence of the gods to continue to love the creatures, these items
had degraded the world into a molten plain of nothing. She walked six thousand of miles.
Her clothing, which had names in the old world, melted away. Her body, which had not
the name of "body," still walked. She walked seven thousand of miles. In all, she walked
seven thousand of miles.

The side of the world that contains all gods, it was melted into degradation. The side of
the world that contains all words, it was melted into degradation. The side of the world
that contains all things, it was melted into degradation. All the three worlds were melted
into a plain of nothing. WOE walked seven thousand of miles.

WOE saw the god SKIN was melted until it was empty entirely. It appeared SKIN was
made of many creatures. There were creatures coming out of SKIN, melting, the creature
who said: *I am beautiful*, he melted, the creature who said: *I ignore every thing I touch*, he
melted, the creature who said: *I need you*, he melted, each one came out of SKIN and

began to desire, and in desiring he melted, until SKIN was empty. And SKIN appeared as a sack with no inside and no outside.

WOE saw the god named STATUE was melted until it died. Formerly STATUE appeared to support the chipping-out of any statue at all. If STATUE was your friend, you could make statues. WOE saw STATUE melt into several smaller gods. One was called WHY, one was called NOT-CARE, one was called DESTROY-ALL.

WHY melted immediately and left no sign. NOT-CARE did not melt even when it died, it did not change shape until it burned finally and blew away in ashes. DESTROY-ALL stayed alive, it would not melt or die. It moved all across the plain, it grew, it became the sky that was gone, it became the earth that was gone, it became the plain. DESTROY-ALL was the plain, it disappeared in that way, DESTROY-ALL was the melting.

WOE saw every word she ever spoke, she saw them. She saw the word "my," she saw the word "flute," she saw the word "give." She saw every word. The words did not live on the side of the world where words live. They were on the plain of nothing and she saw them empty out.

She saw the word "know." The word "know" broke open and spilled out. The word "know" contained many creatures. There was a creature who could not close his mouth. He spoke, saying: *Destroy every thing that makes you unsure.* He melted and died into the plain. There was a creature with no genitals and no hair, who said: *I am very beautiful.* It melted and died into the plain. There was a creature without the ability to think or see, who said: *I dwell in all places, I am everything.* He melted and died into the plain. WOE saw "know" empty, it was like a sack with no inside and no outside. It burned and scattered ashes until it was gone.

She saw items or things rise up to praise themselves. A jar praised itself in its beauty. It said: My maker, the king of all glass jars, made me the most great of all glass jars. I was a free gift of beauty to every future person. I was an expression of the in-dwelling soul of my maker. I was a speech of calm and joy to all persons. I was triumphant, I smashed all other jars, including my brothers and sisters. I was the gathered wisdom of all glass makers. I was more important than the private life of my creator. I was more important than the private lives of those who looked upon me. I was a blue glass jar. I decreed destiny. I ruined men who yearned to make a jar like me. What liquid I contained was only an offering to me. I had no practical purpose. I was the only true meaning in our empty universe.

That is what the glass jar said. WOE saw the glass jar melt and vanish away. She saw all objects melt and vanish away.

So that nothing was. Only WOE remained. At her command, the plain was black, the plain was red. At her command, flowering trees appeared and vanished. At her command, persons appeared, they appeared, they spoke together.

Nothing was here, a plain of nothing.

WOE played with names. Her command brought a shepherd, a royal prince, a monkey equaling heaven.

Then WOE did not know what to do. So her command brought the three creatures into war against each other.

Then WOE did not know what to do. So her command caused the monkey to defeat the shepherd and the royal prince.

Then WOE did not know what to do. So she made the monkey ascend to heaven on a somersault cloud.

Heaven, cloud, monkey, the corpse of the shepherd, the corpse of the royal prince, the unseen sheep, the unseen kingdom, the unseen ancestors of the three creatures, all these were in front of her. She did not know what to do.

So she said: *Then they melted back into the plain.* They melted back into the plain.

She did not know what to do.

She spoke. She spoke names, she spoke the names.

Without telling a story, she sat and spoke the names. Some names she remembered, some names had never been spoken prior.

She only spoke because she was alone, and there was nothing. She was alone, and there was nothing.

She spoke the names, she did not cease speaking.

She spoke the name of barriers, she spoke the name of copper, she spoke the name of dice, she spoke the name of toy birds, she spoke the name of ocean.

She spoke the name of loyalty, she spoke the name of cow's milk, she spoke the name of sexual intercourse, she spoke the name of dysentery, she spoke the name of stone.

She spoke the name of jewels, she spoke the name of houses, she spoke the name of oxen, she spoke the name of yearning, she spoke the name of charcoal.

She spoke the name of bitterness, she spoke the name of fire, she spoke the name of family, she spoke the name of axes, she spoke the name of judgment.

She spoke the name of youth, she spoke the name of wisdom, she spoke the name of stinging flies, she spoke the name of burrowing flies, she spoke the name of war.

She spoke the name of sun, she spoke the name of planning, she spoke the name of knife-throwing, she spoke the name of laughter, she spoke the name of decay.

She spoke the name of work, she spoke the name of lies, she spoke the name of alcohol, she spoke the name of edible rats, she spoke the name of the three worlds.

She spoke the name of rebellion, she spoke the name of snakes, she spoke the name of sleep, she spoke the name of doorless chambers, she spoke the name of mud.

She spoke the name of tree-shrews, she spoke the name of religious hatred, she spoke the name of flooding, she spoke the name of smallness, she spoke the name of cremation.

She spoke the name of cobras, she spoke the name of writing, she spoke the name of the two rivers, she spoke the name of altars, she spoke the name of ashes.

She spoke the name of miscegenation, she spoke the name of faience, she spoke the name of flutes, she spoke the name of mussels, she spoke the name of gold.

She spoke the name of terracotta, she spoke the name of yoni worship, she spoke the name of avoidance, she spoke the name of hymns, she spoke the name of bamboo.

She spoke the name of astrologers, she spoke the name of fishnets, she spoke the name of moneylending, she spoke the name of lightning, she spoke the name of thorns.

She spoke the name of pillars, she spoke the name of clapping, she spoke the name of boats, she spoke the name of murder, she spoke the name of drinking-water.

She spoke. She spoke. She spoke for one thousand and eight hundred days.

She stopped speaking.

She looked at her body. I have breasts, she said, I have glorious arms, I have long legs, I have glorious genitals, I have long feet.

Because she named these things, they joined to her. I am a body, she said. I am become a body, the body's name is WOE. The body will be called WOE.

She looked up from her body. The rest of the world was in motion around her. The plain of nothing was gone, the plain of nothing was become an ocean, a land, a sky, persons piling up chops of wood, woodcocks eating insects.

She named every thing. She named every way of things.

She mispronounced the name "story" when she spoke it. Therefore "story" did not appear. No person or thing was living in a story, because of the absence of STORY.

She named pain, melodramatic speech, revenge, poetry, ending, beginning, chit-chat, also all the other parts of story. All these names lived within STORY, yet STORY did not appear.

Therefore no one made a better speech than he could make. In those ancient times, no person flew through the air. No person did a hundred actions in a row, leading to a final action.

Persons lived and then died in the ancient days. That was not a story.

Within WOE was the word "story." Though she mispronounced the name, she knew the name, she carried it on her back.

WOE walked through the world and looked. She saw every thing and remembered speaking its word. She saw every good and evil thing she had named.

She said the word deterioration, she said the word age, she said the word loss, she said the word forgetfulness, she said the word weakening, she said the word degeneracy, she said the word crumble, she said the word useless. She said the word meaningless, she said the word lonely.

She saw everything she made.

Every word she spoke, it came to her. She wore every word on her back.

She was clad in storms, in blood, in fear, in terror, in destruction. Creator of the world, she created destruction, she created decay.

The bright desert, it came from her mouth. The empty dream, it came from her mouth. The fraudulent love affair, it came from her mouth. The struggle to know, it came from her mouth. The unfulfilled desire for immortality, it came from her mouth. The refusal to understand truth, it came from her mouth. The desire to be normal, it came from her mouth.

WOE created the universe, for what reason? She has created the universe, and for what reason? WOE, the woman, created the universe, for what reason?

She spoke the word "reason," she spoke the word "create," she spoke the word "universe." She spoke those names. Do not ask her a question! Do not ask her the reason she created the universe!

Anti-Music

Prakash Kona

And the Poets—it is those straying in Evil, who follow them

From the Surah 26, The Poets, *The Holy Quran*

The vanity of despair I give to music. In music is death. I give up all that you do not understand when I say things in words not familiar to you. I give up affecting you through music of thought. You've borne my despair long enough to detest the person I am. My art is a lie because it does not carry the scent of void. In despair of youth I made a virtue of affectation. I gave my life to stages on which I acted and reenacted faces that gave the impression of silence. My silence is an affected one. A slave to syntax I am. My cleverness showed in desperation with which I relied on lines made in light from the window of a kitchen. The cleverness that bears the insignia of death I denounce in face of truth. I denounce my obsession with forms. I denounce cruelty of sentimentalism that plagues my waking life. I give up the life of performance that you know what I am in truth.

You're kindness of my uncertain blood. The formless violence of my soul feeds on images. Something in me lives a world of its own. Like music it never stops and I suffer in moments of waking. My despair is poetry and so is my death. Against man I've conspired as a man in search of his body. I wasn't thinking of this body. It lived as an image in my blood. To give up uncertainty of blood is to give up rhythm. I speak as an image that rushes from body to body. I cannot imagine knowing you. Kindness greater than death is life. For you I seek and I weep endlessly. Like a washed piece of cloth I feel dry happiness of the sun in my eyes.

Clouds in red night of a desert hold keys to my character. Vainly I look at stars. I'm a logician against my will. I resort to music to prove that I possess a will of my own. And then comes the whistler in dark. She who is not mine and so much like me in all I imagine. We passed the dark and the long road lay in store for us. We moved without thinking of movement. I never felt a desire to hold anything. They were reflexes of a hand used to the idea of possession. Logic battled void. I stood a spectator. I came out of the morbidly private world of fantasy. The starkness of truth that others inhabited stranger worlds than mine pushed me deeper into unfathomable seclusion. Among women I became woman. A man I never was. Among those who disbelieved in manhood I became a person. Among persons I remained a persona. Among words I stood at the threshold of renunciation.

The question involved the lives of others. The answer had something to do with me. I had nothing to ask of myself. I had something to say for who I am. I was tired of playing a game with the past. The heroism of the perfect man or woman was neither heroic nor perfect. I was begging for a moment in the soul of another imagination less perfect than my fantastic self. Who am I in this void where images dance to the tune of dark? The quiet mind feels the void of things.

I am trying to prove myself that there is no ultimate authority or anything closely resembling that. My soul is at stake. There must be a reason for me to die and never return. It is not hard to reject the comfort of logical explanation in the same way that one may reject wealth. Harder than rejection of wealth is sharing the privacy of one's body. Age imposed honesty upon me or I could've politely lied my way through time. The vanity of passing into memory made me good in that compulsive manner one expects from one that does not act out of faith. Faithless I gestured to an audience of numbers.

The aesthetic moments in a poem come from terrible oppression. The sweetening of dust in a prison cell made me embrace every kind of uncertainty. I lay in the shade of leaves with feet in sunlight. Our worlds sought the stars of night as they descended into dusty tents. We might've been asleep but for that long thought that marched beyond the mountains at the edges of deserts. The waters of that well I drank from one afternoon while my feet falling asleep reverberated in my consciousness. I wasn't dying then. For one that dreamt of escaping rooms it is sad that I should be dying in one as I write these words. I begged my body to let me out for those few moments before the eye shut to music of streets. Purged of the sensation of sound I saw words burn with the fury of wind as it violently struck the sloping canvas of the tent. If I prayed it would've to be out of fear. I would be praying to my fears. Despite the trembling heart reaching my throat I watched my fears. Pain made the body human. I had to find a way outside my humanity.

I ventured outside my quietness to feel the surfaces of things. The element that you never calculated appeared on one of the surfaces. Was the sweetness worth the pain that came from the wave at the edge of being? Pain slept with sweetness of milk in a coconut.

I am incapable of acting illogically—that's the problem with what I am. I wish to make a leap across forms. I want to be a child the same instant that age creeps into my body. The wish is not to escape; the wish is to be liberated. I wish to be liberated from theory. I wish never to use words to explain what words have not brought to being. I dispute the perfectionism of mathematics. Numbers are irrelevant and the suffering of one person is infinite making the presence of a living universe that vibrates to the cry of pain a fact as such. The ears of religion are audible to the cry of pain. Art sleeps when fears of men overwhelm streets. The more I think of music I remember the puff of madness that raises me temporarily from an obsessive gloom into a piercing light. I return as queens to chambers where one withdraws to conceal the face of madness. My body is terrorized by void of excitement. I'm strangely close to dying while in love with the core of life. I cannot burn away just like that. How would I explain myself to my friends!

Stylistic currents mock my hardened skin of a lifetime's sorrows. I spoke little but the voice in me was relentless. I was plagued to listen to that which spoke from within confines of the body. The best in me was conserved. I broke glasses—my own and that of others. To wipe out those traces on water is the job of historian. Water speaks in a way that eyes that weep understand. I've an amazing contempt for realism though not for reality that my eyes produce in despondency of truth. I mocked in order to give myself a face I never had. I kept mockery in vogue. I resolved not to climb trees because I could not bear the tinge of happiness as I watched my house far away. I could be near a cloud. The earth of friendship filled my bones with life. I might be soul in heavens but I'm body in the village where landless laborers gather at dusk to humor the exhaustion of the day's end. I made a habit of never telling the truth simply because it could not be told. The lies of my sane heart resembled truth in odd moments. Conquered by a glance I embraced slavery of friendship. The black holes of possession do not spare the light of intelligence. I resorted to style as a counterpoint to weakness of my grieving hands.

In which phase of darkness was I when the world began. The poor do not cry. Their condition makes tears redundant. Death hangs on their heads without coming close enough. Bread and happiness is religion of the poor. Religions speak in silence of what is not a word. What is bread of the soul but bodies of the poor pilloried by an irredeemable situation! If the wordless religion demands that the poor revolt who then needs words! We owe our bodies to the poor. The character of the sacred is derived from the dark labors of the exploited. The impoverished bodies of the poor that age before their time are forms of my own. Away from my body I authored lifeless fiction where people met and conversed as if to meet and converse was in their nature. My spirituality rejects the music of harmony. Like honey, spirit comes out of bodies of exploited. In their hands *I am what I am*. How could I be spiritual if I never earned my death! Death became sweet as honey of spirit when I became one with those who suffered the loss of spirit having been dispossessed of their bodies. We could be friends in the void—the one who had nothing to lose and the one who had nothing to gain living in shadows of illusion.

I had no song to sing because my throat had dried with unfulfilled thirst of my soul. Where does this caravan move while I barely distinguish between sand and shade! I need salt for my spirit. I need to be nourished of something sweeter than tears. They were not fingers that touched you but words moving in twilight. The dark accentuates my features because I'm not hidden by a face. I displayed austerity despite my blazing eyes coming close to reveal the scars of my heart. My voice could turn a betrayer. I stayed quiet as long as quietness of dark did not threaten to engulf me. I was escaping from a past that had no meaning to the long journey that my feet had undertaken. The shifting eyes of writers of fiction while their heads are constant stayed with me all along. I saw no point writing while something greater than the written word stared in my face. I consoled myself that I was living a curse. The blank heat of days and shadowy nights gave a sense of dying to my unprepared soul. I could've begged for cure but there was none to life me from the anguish of desertion. The bodies I left behind swarmed the desert. I had to die before another word came out of my lips.

When I think of the bodies of poor, they are so many that I am reminded each pair of eyes bears a sorrow of its own. Various destinies bondage has knit them on earth. I suffer periodic bouts of withdrawal from an otherwise placid chair in the sun. In warmth I let water flow into my bones. I gave no cause to worry in a neighborhood anxious of making music out of stones. Their homes last longer than worlds that they dream of. My dreams are born in ashes of time. My music is silence of death and there are no stones to support homes that I imagine. I am weightless other than heaviness of heart that comes from a sense of void. I perform to compensate the loss of a home. Of late my spirit rejects performance. Though poverty is a condition devoid of music no one can humor the bitterness of living like the working classes. I prefer the term 'working classes to the 'poor.' The poor seems a passive phrase if we are referring to the class whose consciousness of living makes the earth go round.

I share the dubious distinction of having never written a single word. I'm not a writer. I could be a performer when it suited the audience too fatigued to respond to the performer's tantrums. I'm performing when fingers move on pages. I'm essentially a translator. What is strange in the languages of others, I sought to bring to the stage of my work as the most obvious of truths. I could be poetic without being a poet. It seems pointless to dream of sounds. Eyeless I gave words the shapes of eyes. I discarded the mask of performance to don the faceless truth of a smile in dark. I dream of real faces of actors. They must be incomprehensible like signatures on carbon papers. I entered temples and the gods absconded. With the stupendous effort that I avoid my listeners, I draw their ears dangerously close to my lips and whisper secrets of my distraught soul. My listeners feel the imposition of a language for none but one. I bear in me the humility of time contra eternity. We're actors in void. Me too. I grasped the twinge of regret that altered the expressions on my forehead. My sense of another person is like a footstep that triggers a sensation in brain. My image of you is not you. That imagined state of an unimaginable you is the center of my performance. I deny the presence of the world I never made. The gardens of senses brought the world into being. The sadness locked in my chest is from a time before I was born. Compassion roots me in a timeless oneness. My world is that of silent lips and articulate insights. I blessed the worm of death cruising the blood for a timeless moment. I remade a world I did not know but felt as if it did not have an existence apart from my own. I believed in you with the instinct that a child takes in sweets.

Art is a fascist that meaningless comfort makes look meaningful. Beauty is a delinquent's seriousness. Music is unmethodical and there is something terribly insincere in metaphors that toy with ideas. To live without thinking, thoughtful as the dark, true to a disposition that is spiritual but not given to subordination of a word, that speaks but does not wait for the writing hand to recollect the unsaid essence, that dances in the instantaneity that one dreams, cuts through fancies but bears the weight of time with the weightlessness of the body in water, such a life does not bow to pray, the living is praying. The resignation with formidable strength on faces of the poor trivializes every other knowledge in comparison. Behind the look of resignation are a variety of lives compressed in slums and ghettos of the world. The intimacies of small places are musical in character. The music I denounce is one that comes in way of dying. That which I call fascist is what postpones the moment of transformation that death can make possible. The weariness I encounter has the power of water. Music born of weariness makes the worst seem unreal in face of time. The bodies of poor have conspired in their own demise to preserve the music of being. This death by music is a phantasm in comparison to hands that lie on the breast of the sleeper. For one quaking in dust, music made things passable. The enhanced worldviews of music come from a drugged state in contrast to loneliness of eyes that wander across landscapes in search of meaning.

Tonight I'm more traumatized than usual. The demons of day have come back with vengeance overwhelming the body of the sleeper. Dissatisfaction married to guilt is the night of life. I complain and there are no hearers. In state-run departments there are endless queues of people waiting to fill forms with tunes of old movies playing from nearby cafés. I wonder what their lives would be like if they had no forms to fill. Sometimes it is raining and we've more to talk about than usual. Desperation is a normal state of mind. Back home the wives must be cutting vegetables and children playing unaffected by dust or sunlight. The happy moments were the way back when we returned to imaginary loves and real homes. Sleep is a drug like a shot staying for a while before departing into daylight. Passionately we await late evenings as if night had something to offer that would take care of the day's miscommuniqués. In dramas of nights we existed for ourselves. The illusion of a self was powerful enough to hypnotize day into a shadow. The descent into poverty of middle classes is the theme I'm most familiar with. I identified myself with the poor. The poor had less to be ashamed of being more familiar with their poverty than I was with myself. There was a bridge of void I had to cross in order to know the poor in their variety as individuals and their oneness of being the exploited. As I reached the point where I had nothing to wait for I saw my life in perspective. My life as a performer had come to an end. The hardest point was my being weaned from view cards of twilight indistinguishable from dawn that I saw outside gray shops with cracks in walls. I must've been a child but to be away from sea is a numbing sensation. I embraced longings and made a virtue of that indefatigable search for a music that combined triumph of spirit with death of body. I failed and the character of my journey changed. I saw that people whom I sought to avenge shared little of tormenting angst that drove me from void to void. The least injured I was first among avengers. I dared to adopt dreams of others as my own. My dreams lay vainly spent on streets waiting for traffic to pass by. I dared to win the war against dust.

The melody of my being has no outlet but dream or despair. I was a victim of words. I made it a habit to turn words against themselves. Friends became foes and beds of traitors produced warmth for soul. I surveyed the platform of eyes that stared at me for no reason. It must be the masks I wear that keep slipping off my face. I make stories to overcome the embarrassment of being seen. The worst embarrassment is my birth in blood and the wailing that made me normal to eyes on platform. I craved the music of anonymity. I transfigured once I knew that the eyes of watchers strayed from my own. I wasn't sufficiently spectacular in a crowd. If I hanged myself in the center of the street I would attract so little attention that the embarrassment of my soul would persist in afterlife. I intend to be tragicomic though I end pathetic. I depend on abstract philosophies to keep my breath going. The more you know me the less you know yourself. In perspective is predilection. In the dilemma of yesterday and tomorrow is my today. In you is the possibility that gave birth to me. The journeys from which I learnt the most are actually returns to points that I might have crossed with or without my knowledge. In effect I know a thing twice in the same moment. Rumination is baseless activity. It proves nothing. My dreams are music but those dramas of possession are in the desire to preserve the turmoil of an age without purpose. The backgrounds that blend all too easily with foregrounds threaten the dream of possession. I repudiate history that comes in the way of my being. I became individualized in the music of senses. The volatility of my nature came from grievances of a heart that burnt in order to burn.

Image gone the stage is a dark place. Replete with shadows sans objects I danced to the tune of reality. I made music out of a thought. I wanted to keep as many faces as my eyes could register. I wanted to leave the protest of my dying face in as many eyes possible. What had I proved to my body except that I was a soul of dust! I moved among men secluded as the shadow of a rose. The feet that walked upon dust and rose petals knew the violence of sea that shook to tremors underground. In retrospection my days were numbered. In anticipation I hoped for more than I could imagine. Either way I had a single point to stand upon that disappeared with every step I took. My voice shook when I remembered. Memory has a way of purifying the cruelest of acts. Histories like historians are impatient to complete. Suggestion is painful and silence overpowers the mind intent on fullness of words. The arrow of future pierced veils I designed in past. There was never a time like 'now.' I'm fussy about slight headaches. Moodiness is in moons of the soul. The middle of a night and I sat meditating on a road. Countless daylights appeared and reappeared and there was no instant to recollect the occurrence.

My life is a palimpsest with each phase erasing previous lives. In my blood is a yearning for quiet. I held my breath to the violence of transformation. The bird from the tree of life fell into the clutches of the predator. The bird chose its way to return. I stuck to the crowded parts of the train where I could travel ticketless. It was a way of return-ing to places long forgotten. I was not free of doubts that plague the faithful. Satisfy anything but the child in my body was insatiable. I had given too much of myself to walls of a prison whose colors were constant. I fell in love with the grayness of time. When moments strike the sensual body locked to a single point imagination drew connections between history and the self. I holidayed from the chains of the present as I let my fancy sweep fields of November through the window of the compartment. Small towns at the crest of villages and wet railway platforms without a shade, a panorama decked for my senses in flotation, weight on my nerves, my exhausted sensibilities, the thickening of a plot with the wild on war with the tame, the eternity I subscribe to is a circle, dragged by dispositions with the force of tsunamis, your times are yours and mine is a correlate to yours in spirit, somebody dies for the dark to express a gesture of conciliation, the feeling of sacrifice is in the blood, the swords of reason triumph to a falsetto, one with bodies at one with nothing, my body had no reason but to flow with matter, spiritual are nameless bodies that work with no music to guide the soul.

The war against uncertainty I'm doomed to lose. The instant I give up treading on thorns I've ceased writing. I calmed the nerves with song and dance. The gods are born of uncertainty. How could I war against the gods without acknowledging my despair! I felt with the smallness of lives that asked merely for sleep free of thoughts. In pain the slightest relief seems like liberation as in killing thirst when a glass of water is all a person would ask for. Denied of a tune to lift their souls crawling in their famished bodies mad crowds turn into mobs. Their souls that dream of escape are given to vacuity. Their music comes from murder. Their murder is a source of terrible joy that sends clouds of smoke into the night air. In fear of uncertain dark I refrained from sacrifice that brought sweetness. I stayed secure from disease, squalor and poverty. They existed without my knowledge and I lived in comfort of their absence from sight. Uncertainty dogged the king that lived on a palace built on a pillar. Death came and I was not ease with my aged bones. I had no answers because I lived a life free of questions. The questions did not go. Neither did the dark hiding beneath eyelids. They came as answers from proud lips. My soul rose in submission to a fight it was unprepared for in the great void of names.

Your family is fine, your children too, your neighbors, the village you come from, your ancestors among trees, lakes, hills and forests, dry leaves and your feet in footsteps of the fox, the friends who wait for you, love that carries the weight of desire like a drop of water streaming down the interior of a teacup, the certainty of numbers is limited to the fact that my mother is sometimes your mother and your daughters are daughters of the village and your sons are jokers that wait for waiting women and my husband's brother's son has thighs strong as a stag and when he sings I hold him in my breath and the girls do the same and he in so many dreams that he can never be one or the same and our lands belong to the dead before they are inherited by the unborn and you can never be certain with buffaloes that could stray but they certainly return before dusk for they like you and I prefer the company of likes and who says that we die because it was never proved that a spirit does not find its way into a bush where it stays until daybreak and the crow takes it and keeps it safe in a nest and on the twelfth day the tree has imbibed the spirit sending it through roots into lake and sea with sand as a faithful messenger and my grandson keeps speaking of me as his mother as I call him my spouse in a different life when I was the tiger on a hill and he a crocodile and we mated and it rained and plants were born and there was grass enough for buffaloes and there was milk enough for the village and there were stars that were milk drops spilt from breasts of goats and the wild rumor began that hill was in love with sea and another rumor more certain than the previous one is the tree that married the most beautiful girl in our village whose ears touched the ground and whose eyes were large as coconuts and whose breasts filled the sky and whose hands held the world upside down and whose nose like that of the buffalo was the dream of every one old and young and children and girls and mothers and sisters and dancers and husbands and fathers and grandfathers and their mothers and spirits that watched and the unborn that were watched upon.

"Book 24: Humble & So Humble"
(from *To the House of the Sun*)

Tim Miller

When winter came I wandered as long as I could before the weather was unbearable: & I somehow always came upon bodies—bodies frozen in fields: bodies dead three days or more, bloated & livid & oozing what bodies are filled with. & I'd sit beside them & stare at the dead arm or dead leg or dead face & then look at my own arm or leg or face & say to myself *This body too will be like that: it is not exempt from that fate:*

or I passed them as they were being eaten by crows or vultures or dogs, or when crawling with worms: & as I watched the teeth or paws or slimy wormskin work itself over the dead arm or dead leg or dead face, I would look at my own arm or leg or face & say to myself *This body too will be like that: it is not exempt from that fate.* & I'd stay with those animals if they would let me: I'd let the worms crawl the length of a finger, if they wanted, & imagine that finger soft & dead—& I'd smell the breath of dead blood & gone flesh from the mouths of many animals, if they'd let me: I'd lean to the mouth & smell what had happened to the body, but not to life:

or the bodies I found were older, much older, behind bushes as if they went to hide those last moments—& as I came upon fleshless bones or bones completely disconnected but still near one another or bones scattered entirely—here a skull & there a shin or part of an arm or leg—I would sit & stare at the white toughness of bone thrown in the white snow: & I would say to myself of my own skull or shin or arm or leg *This body too will be like that: it is not exempt from that fate:*

or the bones were older than that: & no skin clung to a thing: & some of them were beginning to crumble or were already crushed: & some had their skull or pelvis or ribcage caved in or destroyed—& seeing these, I would feel my own skull & press my own pelvis & knock at the door of my own ribcage & realize quietly that *This body too will be like that: it is not exempt from that fate*:

& sometimes in the snow I couldn't tell if what I was lifting was snow or bone-dust, the pile in my hand blew away so easily—& I knew my own body was made to blow away & fly & scatter this way:

& finding unburied human beings I would note that I found them with my eyes: or heard their rattling with my ears: or felt them with my hands & skin—or I approached them with feet that worked & legs that bent & a stomach at ease & no longer sickened by such things: no longer terrified by death: no longer proud of the body & its ability to arise: no longer saddened by the inevitability of its vanishing—of my vanishing & the vanishing of all else: but not life:

& I sat quietly that winter near bodies & bones & former lives & prayed that whoever these people had been or were now, that they not be sad or afraid to be undone, since the rolling rattle of some skull is only natural, & that life only became something else:

& I thought what lessons I could learn from all of them, so still—since, whether newly-dead or sliding from flesh to slime to dust, I could take one of those corpses & try & set it up somewhere—& it wouldn't resist being moved: it wouldn't grumble about its position or protest being sat up or laid down—& if I were to put any of them in new clothes, even the simplest finery would seem strange & unnecessary next to its unmoving humility & stillness—& if I had a chair nearby & tried to make it act like a king: or the owner of a carriage: or the important master of some estate or company, how wonderfully it would refuse, & let its head fall rather than stare up in arrogance—& how wonderfully it might even slide off the chair completely, humble & so humble. There's much for me to learn from a corpse: it does not judge: it does not care being jostled about: it insists on nothing—& somehow I must be the same.

But when it became too cold I had to find the nearest city: & I stayed there to keep warm:

& in the city there are a thousand fires to keep people from the cold: there are fires in every eye for every thing: there are fires in the eyes of every man for every other man who might have more or want more than him: there is a fire in every eye for every new thing: for every new gun or saddle or shirt or boot: every new machine or invention or mere rumor: there is a fire in every eye that passes over the newspaper & the mailman with a leering expectation & a horrified suspicion—& with these fires they keep themselves occupied:

& there's the fire of delusion & the fire of the senses that burns all of them with every feeling that comes from what they see & hear: every impulse that comes from what they see & hear: every ambition that comes from what they see & hear: every sight & sound they see & hear that sends them off in some other direction entirely, forever—& with these fires they keep themselves occupied:

& there's the fire of hatred & the fire of boredom that combine one evening when two drunk women become enraged with one another: & as they begin to call & curse, every other man & woman forms a ring around them & adds their own voices: & they pass both women a few knives each: & they cheer to watch a desperate fight, enthralled at the body & its ugliness, at how easily it's torn & how stupidly these women stoop to destroy themselves—& with these fires they keep themselves occupied:

& there's the fire of the eye & the mind & of justice when a man murders a horse-thief: & the horse-thief's fellow thieves murder him: & the city finishes the affair by hanging the thieves—& those with fire in their eyes & in their guts come out on a frozen day to watch the men suspended from the lengths of frozen rope, burning & warm with the fire of their own satisfaction—& with these fires they keep themselves occupied:

& there's the beautiful & seemingly indestructible fire of enchantment: beautiful enchantment & gorgeous enchantment with bodies & the sounds of attractive voices: bodies & the smell of food: bodies & the sounds of a new floor or a horse at full-gallop & the tremendous energy that comes from speed & wonder & movement: bodies & the addiction of movement & sound: bodies & the addiction to new movement & new sound & new enchantment with every new thing: bodies & the addiction to perpetual motion: bodies & the energy of friendships & bodies & the energy of the supreme & wondrous enchantment that *A mountain is there & I must go to it*—& with these fires they keep themselves occupied:

& there's the fire of pride when one night a poor man comes through the crowd: & his palms are out for begging: & he's thrown a few coins before they begin to laugh: & from all sides are a half-dozen voices of laughter, watching as he goes: & they remember together how long he's been begging here—& I walk past them mute with anger & give him the shoddy coat I'm wearing & say "Friend, remember me: you gave me this coat when I needed it: you should take it back." & he looks at me, delirious with cold, & wraps himself & goes on his way:

& only a few of the crowd even saw what I did: & I wanted to say that all things are only a loan till we find someone poorer than ourselves—but it took all I could to pass them & come to the first alley & throw up for sickness. Because the worst fire comes from the eyes of others: the fire of being seen & being heard & being smelled: the fire being felt & tasted & judged: the fire of renown & the fire of shame: the fire of fame & the fire of power: the fire of love & fear & the need for all of it to come from everybody—the fire of an enflamed mind that wants to own or buy or sell or kill or organize or fix or destroy the entire world—& with these fires they keep themselves occupied:

because there are the fires of small-pains & small-pleasures: & the first is avoided while the second is sought, yet both are the same & each yields the other: & I watch or listen as it happens, as they avoid small-pain & so find small-pleasure but end up with small-pain in time—or its opposite—& they burn in their run towards small-satisfaction: & they burn in their run from small-disappointment, not seeing the road they run on is a circle that comes to one or the other eventually—& with these fires they keep themselves occupied:

& as the winter begins to wane all these fires become one when an Asian woman named Mary is burned so the gold she has can be distributed to others: & there's the fire of greed for her gold, & the arrogance that assumed others deserved what she had: & there's the sad fire of fear—always at risk of being snuffed out, it's so weak—that gold & recognition is all there is: & there's the sad fire of desperation that wants the eye perpetually surrounded by gold: golden sights & golden sounds & fellow people made of gold—the streets paved in it & the buildings painted in it & the sky encrusted in it—& there's finally the fire of a man I saw in a vision, holed up in a hotel & barricaded in a room stuffed with gold & women—yet stuffed with these so much he couldn't move to make use of any of it, & barely had enough room to survey his world & worry about it:

& the dead Asian woman set on fire burned slowly as the winter went away: & by morning a path of ashes led from the post where she'd been tied down the street & around the corner, to tell you how the wind had been blowing. & looking at her I had to wonder where her gold came from—did she burn someone to get it? & why did she want gold in the first place? & is everyone who runs after gold merely waiting in one line or another—those who burn & murder & steal, & those burned & murdered & stolen from—merely waiting for their turn to come up? Is this what fire does?

& those who do these things are like men convinced they can only create heat & light: & they gather all the wood from every forest & pile it high & set it on fire & marvel at the fire they've made: & they marvel at their ability to create light: & they're amazed at the light & heat & energy they've created—all this while they can't see the other side of their fire, it's so large: they can't walk around it to see the other side, it's so wide: & after awhile they can't conceive of another side or another light or any other kind of life—& they spend their lives feeding this awful fire: & at some point it's so high & so bright & so hot it blinds them, though by this time they wouldn't know:

& this actually happened once, to a group of men previously of such great charm & such great capacity for food & drink & life—& one evening drunk & worshipping themselves—one evening drunk & worshipping the music of the mandolin & piano & the drunken songs, they ran into the midst of a huge bonfire—one evening drunk & worshipping the women who surrounded them & the men who envied them, they ran into the streets ecstatic with their own stupidity & ran into a fire as if they were a fire—as if they could leave the fire—as if the fire could not touch their skin, backed up as it was by gold & some great reputation—& the three men ran into the midst of the fire & collapsed there—& they never screamed, only burned, unaware.

& where are the people who enter the fire completely aware: & where are the people who walk through it completely aware: & where are the people who emerge completely aware? Where are the people for whom fire is like water, who ignore the flesh of their faces &

the palms of their hands & how their legs look while walking—where are the people who drown in the fire & survive? Watching the residue of any flames I realized I didn't know—& when the fire was out no one could say where it had had gone—east or west or north or south—since it simply wasn't there. Whenever this happened to a person they simply weren't there: but I was still here: & this made me feel terribly alone.

& I left the city as the world became warmer: & I came upon the dead as before, but couldn't watch them as before: couldn't sit with them as before: couldn't see my own bones or arms or limbs the same as I did theirs. I could say that *I will one day be like this* but couldn't feel love for those who probably never said this: who lived by their bodies & died by their bodies only. The people I passed winter with in the city showed me this, & something like hatred filled me:

& if I were to take each body—dead, now—& talk to it: whisper to it: speak to it: if I wasted all my breath on a pile or a field of bones, would it do anything at all: would my breath fill those bones & give them life again: would it bring flesh back to those bones: would it give skin to those bones—& if I said to the wind or the rain or the receding snow *Cover & fill these bones with your breath*—would it mean a thing: would they rise again & live another life—or would they only lie there, still dead & hopeless from the life they'd lived? & would it matter, if rising meant being consumed by the fire again?

But then one day I came upon an animal in the middle of a field: & the field was still dead & it waited with patience for spring—& at first I saw the animal & thought it was eating one of its fellows. It looked starved & ravenous & went at the body before it as if it might never eat again—but then I saw its head only, floating there, the light blue of dawn between the bottom of the head & the ground—& I realized it had eaten its own body & consumed its own flesh until there'd been nothing left to eat. & in this open field dead from the winter I saw the floating head of this animal suddenly squirm & become the full-body of a large hawk, who did the same: & I watched it begin at its feet & consume its own belly & eat its own wings until only its narrow head & wise eyes & beak remained. But then the bird's head too seemed to shiver or squirm, & in a moment its head extended & elongated & became the body of a human, sitting there with his legs crossed: & in a strange display he actually shivered in the cold—the wind did bite—before looking down at his feet: & he lifted one to his mouth: & he stopped & saw me & said "This is what happens so long as I breathe & move:" & he slowly & considerately & with admirable patience & exactness removed the skin from one foot & ate it—& when there was only bone left where the skin had covered it, he merely took a few minutes to crack it off, toss it to the side, & begin on the other: & then to his legs: & upwards as far as he could, until only his floating head remained. & I thought *This body too will be like that: it is not exempt from that fate.* & I watched this all night with love & fascination:

& as spring came on I walked the road the mailmen used: & the mailmen & the rest flew by with a feverish ardor as if they could not go quick enough: as if they were assured they would never die yet still worried their life might end before they could relish every moment. & they're all kindling, galloping & breaking away into the burning distance.

& I came to understand where I stood when one evening in a vision I saw a pillar of fire in the sky: & it seemed to extend to the stars: & while many ran from it, I ran towards it: & I wanted to climb it, if I could, & carry others with me—but when I got there a man was in the fire already with his arm out to me: & his other hand held that of another in the flames, & I saw a spiral of people wound around up to the sky's edge, their faces orange & gold.

Into the Desert

Cameron Pierce

When Freud slipped out of a tree he said, "This way to my father's house."
So Jung took the path through the jungle
searching for Kurtz or some other fellow.
It was there he found his shadow eating mangos by the river.

I was tripping in the city that consumed Gregor Samsa
when the desert called me up and said, "This is urgent,
the snake doctor's shopping umbrellas in the fungus garden."
So I bolted from town and on the way
dragged my shadow through a puddle of Rorschach rabbits.

This is Egyptian civilization in California,
King Tut tuning in under a scorpion sun.
Everyone goes insane in the desert.
It's extraterrestrial.
Freud, I'm surrounded by joshua trees and you're one of them.
In the mind's jungle, cockroaches scheme
behind motor homes driven by God's crippled violin
and that lunatic choir of billions who chant all together
in the key of future illusions.

Hurry up now, history is meeting us on the mountain.
"It's holy," someone says.
The twentieth century races up in a Corvette and mutters,
"All your gods are dead."
So we change our plan and scuttle into caves of red rock

where the desert collapses *into* us
like this is one of Lovecraft's nightmare conspiracies
and the grand invasion called modern life
is about to take a second giant leap.

I promise to breathe if you just get Antoine Roquentin and
that thief Genet to leave the room.
These limbs can no longer hold so many dead faces,
not when the path is a one-way road.

Strawberry Airplane
Cameron Pierce

So what if the birds eat all the strawberries?
I don't recall them charging us for the dream of flight,
and we will never know how many strawberries
went into the creation of every airplane alive today.

The Problem with Angels
Cameron Pierce

The problem with angels
is that they are always bumping heads
with other angels.
Shostakovich knew this.
Symphony No. 14 proves it,
            at least in this poem,
            and it's almost as if these lines
            are bumping heads.

Plugged in Somatic

D.D. Wildblood

Torsos, a naked kind of leather scared and attrited. Grapple-batons, absent blades, scissors and sickles in the shadows of these bodies. Cyphers and memories / bruises and scars. Khaki shredded, a bemused logo, rags upon hides / upon sides / portions of meat in mud. Of this image / of wrestlers that flog the canvas / of the campaigns released in the face, full / square in the face. The ID and its new wave language, urban after-hours issue and glossy strands of an attitude inserted in black rubber of embossed body-armour.

Base launched collection. Bullshit upon the urban, broken as drugs, sex and counterfeit goods. Launch recovering line being out there creative behind the attitude putting across product. See the torsos challenged, suck in a sense directly into the beat / pulse / lock-up the zygomatic arches. Parts, tongue / cheek, I think through spattered mud. All have pickings / faces polite / passive as carrion. Though drug-reality in today's. The brutality talks / and the market trades in somatic waste. The sectioned corpse framed as a nasty portrait, toothless and vacant, over-written and impaled. Image suckers see the read caption, short tongues rock idly in privileged mouths.

Sky bleached hot. Cheek punctured by regardless branding / cauterization of soft face. The remains of a torso, the image shot engages and the khaki a secondary integument still burns / melts, rivulets score channels in desensitised flesh. The gratification / identifying a generation / a opus of patients swallowed in the syndromatic models, calculated to provoke endemic triumph of cause and motives.

It is still and all remains questionable, rot, the innocent degree of knowledge assumed on the journey from black boot dancing to the director of the agency / ballerina limbs dance in the mud. Psychological effects on a formal night going ready where possible / encountering fantasies and agencies learned of the punches when speaking. Commands, orders violence static ricochets in helmet / wire frame overlay, smeared accompaniment on visor.

Promoting drug launch, a scent fusion puked into the sky.

Company took out the back of ID's skull and inserted folded programming.

Stood speed-wrap / ID inside wrap perfume a fusion sniffing the message of used and crumpled language. Crucially ID's reader still condemned promoting a censoring of the initiating revival.

Brittle Head

D.D. Wildblood

Hand imprinted by rubber / a happy aspect and linear impressions in the palm / immaculate fascistic violins spawn scission / the soporific pains / the emasculated fountains that spout an ignorance of fast food and yet can't cook / more comfortable with their tractors harvesting food / the 11:27 from where the dog shits behind its notice board prison / from where the ammunition passes through / strapped down / in metal cases and clearly labelled / I fill an underused bin with boredom bottles / smoke down my skin in ages / in pregnancy harm and inhibited gasps / blood boards the number 10 to rattle along under big skies / underneath thin clouds burnished by the half moon / a screaming white stiletto piercing a waterbed / beautiful gaps in forward teeth / sheaths of thin rubber ruben thighs / tight / circulatory restrictive hoops / ribs / pendulums marking time in erectile tissue / blood strewn hope / hungry veins / happy veins beneath a tan synthetic / a calf muscle bulges and nervous laughter erupts across a volkswagon driven by people in stripy pyjamas...

Provincial Spleen

D.D. Wildblood

Bazaars / mardi-gras and other scenes of bustle and chased confusion / silenced bullets sunk stealthily into the head / the hollow of an empty busy shop / streams of the storyline defragmented / left idle like the happy mad / rainbows in puddles / pools of puke in school corridors / slip in / in gripless tan market boots / the poverty of tolkein until I found Baudelaire / provincial spleens cursing the wind / idolising the dirty verges and detritus between destination / and the repetition of decorative suicidal thought / and the inaccurate regimens of NHS therapy / drugs / solitude / a hand always ready to ease the stiffness / to ease the passage of turnips threatening a rectum / and other suchness / likening likeness to like / to similes of the other / its head and thought / separately going on / wearing T-shirts too tight for its copious belly / with mottos too small so that you might be accused of staring at beer tits rather than reading the witty legend / and how offensive it is when the ugly smoke / cancer gathers in my lungs and seldomly used throat / cut as it is with cheaper white powders / I languor after her legs / faked and drawn to a point / in ballet boots and grease paint / tangents / a cigarette has broken my line / lured me into her arms / her fetal bath / luke warm and fizzing with hair at the nape of the neck / on the bus / over her shoulder and in her third person I read the text she quickly and expertly thumbs into her phone / haha me 2 / send / her spots and moles appear radiant / puss oozes out my left nostril / I take the left hand option and pick up broken pieces of jewellery / it goes in my key pocket in the hope of unlocking something…

Living for a Nuclear Tomorrow

Forrest Armstrong

O fists punching through glass soil your asphalt fingers loom like desolate mountains
      before me

Your eyes staring distant in oceans like crows dotting twilight sky

Your heart a trembling satellite feeding cosmic veins to stimulate numb cybernetics

You would have me to wind as you would a puppet so even my speech belongs to you

So even the words I give to this lined parchment become your shadowed blasphemies

O metallic puppet yourself who must have risen from the hot of the earth's stove I would
      sooner snap my tongue

Eater of seeds of God gardener of metallic forests

What will your world look like when you have given your last monument lungs?

Do you yearn to turn the sun black? Do you yearn to erase the stars?

Do you even realize a future in which every rock shivers with cold electricity?

Instantaneous—as if building a beautiful today will prevent the tomorrow of rot

Junky pumping your veins with oil and eating the bed you sleep in

You could not even dream the cracked mountains obscured as you are by yourself

O figure must stop to wonder who I am addressing

Perhaps a part of myself—a statue built of the ugliness within all human beings

I am tired of belonging to the dollar I would burn everything around me if I could do so
      without starving

I am always starving—the dollar is not enough

I have romantic dreams of myself apart from all this but even in my dreams no food finds
      warmth in my stomach

Still would remain naked in poverty before wearing the glove of the dollar

Gas mask salaries building brainsick staircases into the quiet peak of space

Silicon millionaires at the edge of death looking back and wondering if they've ever lived

Greed! Lust! Living immediately and pretending reality ceases to exist with yourself!

Figure who I will call Mankind, you have webbed me within your elements.

(When I peel the shell off this egg I find myself in the yolk)

I feel as if all I've felt I've felt within a dream—

Everyday wake to find from the cable lines hanging mechanical stars!

I consider the nature of a planet which is in any case a construct and consists of a celestial
        body revolving through time

Did the man who put the flame in these electric windows think of that? Are all the planets
        in space not enough?

Though Mankind in considering motives I find you just as confused as myself

Every time I turn on the television, some new deformity of man staring from behind the
        glass

Return to dreams of erasure but again in my dreams of logic there is nologic

As if amputating one control station could bring the whole network down

No Mankind call me a morbid poet but I do not believe a ticket exists back to the lush

I believe at best we must build a new lush though as always I am screaming these words
        only to the bent trees around me

If I appear to speak to you it is because I am trying to tell myself I am not speaking to
        myself I know you would not be there to listen

What would it take? I offer not answers only idyllic visions of a child (for I am and hope
        to forever remain a child)

(for in child nologic there is purest logic)

Infantile, though I would like to break today in half and emerge from the remnants
        tomorrow, naked and ignorant as if Adam and Eve never bit that apple

Choking in a nuclear greenhouse, detonation in black suit power camps, slaving to the
        dollar, squinting in automobiles wondering which road will show me a bed to
        sleep in, creating new realities from papier-mâché, (fearing anarchy as I praise it),
        men of chemical, railroad stations at the edge of eternity, fractured ground split from
        one coast to the next by hungry animals looking for oil to drink

Tired of turning my stomach every time I read a paper tired of bombs tired of blood spilt
        over nothing tired of country boundaries and laws tired of speech which does not
        belong to me of being an unwilling puppet to a universe of synthetics and digital
        skies

Tired of watching the gears drop from eternity's clock! Tired of belonging to a sky which
        does not look the same across the sands of all galaxies!

Mankind I would give you my knowledge if you would stop sending rockets into space!
And without fear of getting my hands dirty would reach up to rub centuries of grease
    from the antique sky! Ah!

Untitled

Stephen M. Wilson

I

1

US

wee

child

wren fly

Heaven Bound!

love soar; feat/wing.

Angel-birds dive; surface breaking

Ordered pair, Matter/Anti-matter: Morning Glory Mantra

Phoenix ashes dust snail-shell—COCO-DE-MER
A kiss from pomegranate lips betrays my blame.

Me why? Know—not the powers of three—9—
Blame not my y—broken X, fault umbilical of
Chi Lotus. Phallus not my choosing (though would)!
I also ROAR!

Calculate: X+X=SHE…is woman/princess; Frog prince, I?
Kiss, or catch a fly? Fly children, we won! Fly child, wee one—
Burst forth flowers of dawn!
Choose Man. Fly Phoenix, burst like Sunflower from Hell—Heaven bound
Betray not, my lips.

Death smiles, patient of Nature's patterns
Ordered pair, Adam/Eve…do Angels matter?
Back is breaking; feet sore. A rib strayed from my side
Heaven bound but cannot fly!
Wretched children, we/us/one/me
BETRAYED!
Days numbered like Fibonacci.

Slow Burn

Stephen M. Wilson

In a Pollock Rorschach
of imagination
the blood-egg burst
and the beast
looses its heart-beat

I swim to the surface
of the pink embryonic sea
the cutting of new teeth
are sharp against cord
loosening it from Adam's apple pi

Is this the mathematical equation
of an iconoclast—
tasting your soul, blacked
and crisp, yet
lazy like a summer breeze?

I rise through moist flames
origami phoenix
twisting and turning in upon myself
as my other me pulsates
loosing a soul that is now mine.

Death-in-Life Love Song

Kevin L. Donihe

he raises silver
to plow red furrows
through warm peach
resistance

(force + pressure
= oblivion
colored rivers
flow over
safety glass smile)

pulsing rhythm
sings red tides
under hand

(painted lips
sown between
velvety walls
grin without source
only darkness lies
in empty cavities)

death-in-life love song
resonates through
organic strings

(grave dirt

pistons valves

the seat of love

cradled in new

cathedral

he bows

unworthy supplicant)

play these notes

filtered through

foreign blood

— medicinal miracle

pulsing warm reminders

in his hand

Items #6600-6617 & 0930

murmurists

These few sentences... *fist of rational viz mystique*, 'leaps of conclusion', or so on. Today, this is all there is, just more

1. Dandruff of the Orator.

Continue please...

1.1 On on onward, triste of tag wheel, id solar id solar id solar, lights upon, what? Knowledge?

1.2 Logic repeats rationale judgements, 'judgements irrationale,' judgements nonetheless.

1.3 New experience forms essentialism, but is neither essential nor quasi-essential; it is, instead, knowing.

1.4 Absolution changes thought. Such execution promises end-result, but wrongly so. Ha.

1.5 Will is process. (See how they run.) Wilfulness may only be ergo anon, however.

1.6 Tradition implies consequence; tradition implies limitation. Consequently, we traditionally limit.

1.7 That said, reluctance goes beyond some limitations, implying some direction.

1.8 Components of this concept are works of art.

1.9 Ideation is physical. In other words, baby, let's get physical.

2. Blind Networks (of some Bach Utensil 911).

Do not necessitate me, please; proceed in order to set unexpected directions. Can you? I am ideas in the mind. Are you? Can you afford your formalities? I understood my conduct was in question; yet you said little in person. It may never reach a viewing, I know, but may we induce something soon? My ideas pull upon your chain, as you said previously. I share something like the same concept; and since no formality is intrinsic or expressive, that might be enough. For instance, if maths then literature; if literature then maths.... See,

I am concerned only with grey exception. The past applies all over me and how I am....
Meet me at the alter, please.

(OR/ crisisian tempt to all, exempt ....no-one waiting. [strokes ..'ch ch ch change is
[b'jesus man's desiring [understating.

**3. aporial. sweet aporial. triste of sealight, i c u. aporial. sweet aporial. triste of
gaglight, i c u.**

(Proposition: I sign in order to Be; that is, I sign in order to signify Being.)

3.1   End-Spirit: Body affirms Earth; ergo, body affirms region: If so, it follows that spiri-
       tual development is corporeal development. In other words, get some exercise.

3.2   Philological-End-Spirit: I stress bodily development. Likewise, I stress the eroticisation
       of this development. Put the ego in pain——or pay the price. Many are offended by
       this, I know. They lie in gutters of their own making. They work for furniture.

3.3   Their Static Lists Reject You...What Now?: You are offended by your exclusion; yet,
       it is the making of you and your greatest weapon. Divide further; ruthlessly divide.
       Make division your means of expression.

3.4   War Eroticises Pain; Peace Eroticises Life: Not so. You are asleep, and no-one is
       watching over you. Recordings are made of you, but these are immediately erased,
       with their cases stabbed onto spikes in public places.

3.5   Society?: ...At Best, We See Hubs of Personification: We create your reality and your
       opinions, by importing fantastic places into us. See our fountainheads. For us, you
       function as the people we are to love.

3.6   A Suspect Human Nature?: Indeed this is so. People tend toward corruption. In light
       of this, we are authoritarian, in seeing all these tendencies as disconnections from
       reality. Our abstractions defy testing. Attempt no contrast, please.

3.7   The Universe is Unnatural: You crave the ability to distinguish yourself from this, we
       know. You merely play at fighting, however.

3.8   Stereotype Your Enemy: You have basic mistrust——which is good; but this needs
       guidance. Corruption is a science which is itself corruptible. In celebrating this
       diversity, you fail to impose uniform values. Pure authority, and its attendant
       hostilities, brings reason to impersonality.

3.9   Impersonality Presumes Uniformity Anew: The virtue of this is direction. History
       values systems. We favour inquisitions and purges, and evangelise same.

Zoom In

John Moore-Williams

amputee's embrace amidst (slagheap city bared rebar of buildings twisted into nervetrees) a battle between cannibals (rough singing of limbgrind twisting, interweaved, growing in blackblood pool)

cast for broken bones (the slagheap
shudders, distant heartmurmur of steelbeasts'
growling passage),

dictionary of tongues' (dreams)
escape into that (darkmatterbody, wombs of stars whispering the curve)
flesh everyone has worn (outerworn, splitting, at fingertip's softly bladed insistence)

gaping wound of mouth's (shadowcavern awrithe with light)
hiss between rosaries of teeth (distanceglimmer)

instinct of torsos (sing an ice-age-ending heat)

just a (gloss on the endless fritterings of idle hands)
key to bodies without locks, such a (eye-rhyme of hollows)

lonely way to live (an eaten imminence of the remembered)

morsel, sticky-sweet (recombinant
neck's nape, where we hide kisses' genuflections
orange, round and pored of intimacy)

patient (inmates of a decimated land-question asked in touch and haste (scape)

a rage of (neatly
a silence (expounded

ticket to a run-down carnival where
urgency of fingers
violence of hips
wound an air shaped like

xylophone's quiet harmonics
yearning toward yourself, a
zoo full of domesticated beasts

Our Eyes Meat Over the Slaughter

John Moore-Williams

articulate (*what? the echoed husk*
has uttered) of never
      the musk
of memory a long-healed
scar the long pink muscle ruptures
moistening the mouth's arroyo

red net (*the slow member's lonely missive*) timely ripped
,hectic and terse,
a lobotomized muse autonomically muttering
     ecumenical names,
        or the dumb litany of dna
eructation's tarred and etiolated
        yet ardent foam
a thread sore and teething
with ague's knot (*more ineradicable than gordian's*)
monosyllabic as I
     segue's tender naïf
,hot and contiguous,
     'gin old sleeve's id. woeless the decalescent
necessity, a night lingeringly Gnostic and idle,
a thousand hours' descendant
        birthed again and shed, your absence an anemic typo, an ought
near all, popular axiom's sugared coat.

a lilting list defiled (*is deified*), fuming with hot ears yesterday,
now a melting somnolence, erupting in a tamed umbra,

a named pear molting an age of tear and frost.

the hectored keel names you a taut seizure,

an aubade, an echo log, I a voice you wrote,

                                                    seized,

your Alba on a pillory, sere, usurious, a yelp

neither of wildernesses nor yet yours,

a city of unhabited towers. a country of crepuscular silences.

            a swarm of tongues.

                    you, o, mouthing

                            whys: a library where countless bodies

lay

prostrate

                                                    stacked cordwood

cordially yours

                                                    for the molten

tongues.

The Nikkeo

Lynn Stongin

The Nikkeo

Neo-natal intensive care unit
gleams in the frost moon.

Head of the night-nurse
sleek as the taxidermist's
stuffed loon.
A Memoir: *A Tremor,* she is writing
    who fled hurricane Rita
        to wind up in the oncologist's office.

        the hive of her head
        hoarding honey
        like bees humming:

Flooded with victims from parishes in New Orleans
    the cancer specialist is blunt, a heavy-hitter
bright as winter stars.

She is trying to hold back death, the poet: with a hook:
with sandbags   with coal sacks;   anything:
with old scars, salt-cellars all shoved up against the caving shoulders of life:

Expanse of wall white as a neck.
Subsisting on love   she & her partner agreed to sign papers
    then drive away   one rainy day.

II.

"Chemo-Brain?"

Caitlin writes (rain-wet pages I take to the coffee-house, bring home to open in lamplight.)

She still has hair:
it's a disappointment that she'd old when
likely to turn bald:
when skin doesn't define hills & valleys of the skull so well.

She's always had an interest in seeing herself bald:

Will she cull wigs, or turbans?

Perfect fall weather.
Stepping outside   almost translucent.

Waiting in the wind-tunnel created by 2 tall buildings is another thing.
Some kind woman who runs a prayer ministry took pity; offered a ride

just when Metro-Cab, for sick people came, 60c
so she reloaded portable oxygen, Bolivian shopping bag with book & hat.

III

Cape Cod: **Silent Like After Snowfall Reflected in Glass**

It's silent like after snowfall reflected in glass:
Cape Cod   the blue lights revolve:
early winter, light bulbs burned like honeyballs. Those were the years.

When you killed the engine, everything turned blue
the old vicarage house

windows reflected fire.

In Europe, one gets good string bags, totes. Why not here?
You shudder remembering grabbing a flashlight from the nail it hung on,
shoving it deep into the apron pocket in Penobscot & Pawtucket.

You hived honey   papery wax combs:

Lining up honey jars   flicking on cast-iron latch to the broom closet &
switching another on the iron-banded door to your wine cellar.

Clicking the flashlight
over the windowless tiny cell (by the boiler room) at heart of your home.

For three-hundred years, this space had not been warm.

The bee had a fast-forward eye.
Virgil's blunt-faced bees.
Your eye is de-railed. You feel it unspool.

Look at the shoulder-gun shone by sun.

    You too were silenced then behind closed gold glass
    Knowing no matter how bad things got
    you could always find your way by the moon.

IV

Christchurch   Churchstone

Stubborn spire of Christ church
organ pipes like bones of ice.
"The Lord is our strength," said the tiled floor of the movie theatre, The Roxie.

She'd taken her poppies, last autumn, lifted a match to their waists

locked them off

burned black as they were

to keep them from bleeding to death: stanched, a stump, am amputation.

Needle-sharp

the steeple pierces opaque sky.

The window back then when she drove to the Cape Cod library was a convex transparency.

Wrens erupted from the winterbush.

Swaddled in reindeer-hide

forehead daubed with soot

the writer performs.

V

There's a disconnect.

She flashes back to that time her first born was in the Nikkeo.

Now the loss is your own

body & beloved blood & bone.

Beginning to feel the confiscation,

"I am starting to feel the death of everything I had. I miss my waffle-maker.

Am I going to leave this earth without ever having flax waffles again?

Always been a bit of a theatre bird

Always been a foodie.

Good Euro-French food. Greek."

Container-truck drivers are striking   silver oils the night:

Soft-wood lumber workers   going back

making a strange circular diagram from sky. making

special patterns in black rain, white snow.

You never knew a person could cry so much.

Christchurch is lit now in the hour of your loss like a stone lantern geometry & grief one glow.

V

Down in South Texas High (writes Caitlin) the very brightest students were
hand-picked   given classes with full professors   making
special patterns in black rain, white snow:
advanced work
privilege.
For instance, when in gym, they didn't have to wait in line.

Well, Texas and a very small town:
the need to have this: Two different water fountains, bathrooms
for black & white youths
there down South
in Friendswood.

Conditions in her present valley?
Mostly, my friend walked in the green green mountains of Costa Rica
(writing her Memoir, *Tremor,* recalling)
and cried over losing Nai Gong.
A crucial time:
marble-floored, French-windowed, balconied little houses dominated the horizon.

Mountains made clouds every day so it could sometimes rain in afternoon.

Luckily, it wasn't rainy season so Cait could walk every day in the mountains.
"I never knew a person could cry so much."

Now, coming to the beginning of the end,
will she revise that statement?

VI

Architecture.

Interesting architectures:

balconies of hope, she recalls, built onto day: Step out French windows, back into

rooms slowly, eerily.

She went to church:

at a certain point in the service

the priest turned wafers and wine into blood & body   they rang

the church bell.

Tears streamed down her face:

People took notice thinking her very devout. Some tried to sit near her.

Strange event in the little church on the main plaza of Dues Rios

spread in declivities running like wounds into the mountains,

main businesses & regular houses were built in mortal fashion

around it

like protection around a wound.

The Capital drained

emptied out by six o'clock each afternoon.

Everyone desired to live in these high mountains   their astounding greenery.

    What did they do at night?

    There were very few restaurants, clubs, movie houses.

VII

She projects nobility, honor, fame upon the screen of the daily now, in that South Texas town:

Death with his marble scythe approaching

180 degrees opposite to what her parents thought,

her mother entertained an African American in her living room.

    Let stepping outside be miraculous again:

    Over brambles, the wound-gashed mountain   the sound-slashed thunder:

    One can always find one's way   *by the char of the sun,*   *by the moon.*

Passing
C.J. Duffy

whore like radio.

propoganda by dull inches.

diatribe for disaffected.

experience deletes.

my furniture becomes you.

trail like snail saliva.

you listen nonetheless.

silver as outside.

heat from a handglove.

plastic vases and such.

horror of houses.

televisual entrapment.

coal fires as family.

a time before buses like a rumble of markets.

not cold, not distant.

hour glass memory.

fades for the weatherman.

rose petals like razor blades.

I'm not looking for forgiveness,

This tunes not yours to sing.

Fat Finger

C.J. Duffy

disproportionate use of elegance
stylised impulse fails as narcotic
a daisy chain falls from blue skies
deeper the depth of despair
but

you go on and on drawing breath
as a human reverse bellows
filling your pointless lungs with air
when smoke would benefit results
nicotine

stains your intellect and spoils fingers
highly polished glass fronts
glaze the world a distant away
but never far enough
to remove the trace of human remains

cold the heart of our culture
that wraps its legs around your
flacid flesh the better to constrain
your doleful, woeful natural needs
as

living portrays the dead as losers

All to Mud
C.J. Duffy

hat sank. fallow field. the poppies blossom with the crucifix. bones of history bleached. dull mud. bricks and bottles and dun land. the sky brings a compromise. a heavy damp weight. playing cards chase players. smoke now clings to frayed photo's. time lacks evidence. explosions echo in foreign lands. the dead laugh. the dying. unbelieved. unbelieving. repeats as tarnished promises. and on. anon.

A Life in the Day

Jeff Mock

Ja, hello, good morning. My name is Franz,
But you may call me Herr Stukker. At dawn
I rise to hang myself, and find the rope
Is frayed. So, on to the menace of breakfast.
After which I reset my jaw and brush
And shave my fingerprints away. The swirl
Of water down the drain leaves only me.
At work all day I slaughter pigs. It is
Like opening letters. Fond memories—
A flood, a trickle. Ja, think what you will,
But I do not like you either. At noon
I hide in the alley and crunch a brick,
And eat it, and eat another. I eat
A wall. I eat an entire tenement,
Light bulbs, saucepans, TVs, cradles, and all.
It is not enough. Bah, who needs work when
All the city is built of brick? You, too,
Your heart is nothing more. But I, I am
A blade and in the afternoon I slit
Another thousand pigs. I am a blade.
I am a shard of glass. I am the safety
Razor that isn't safe. I am the humane
Guillotine. I created France, and what
In return did I receive? I forget
Myself: I am Franz. Once I was a pig,
Or so I once thought. At day's end I let,
For compassion's sake, one fat pig go free

And hone my knife to make tomorrow quicker.

There are too many throats. Some soon day

I will hone its edge to air. At sunset

I sheath my knife and sing it—*la*—to sleep.

I know this knife is far too good for me.

Then it is tomorrow. I rise at dawn

And count the pigs who live, and don't know why.

Bless me, I am Franz and human by birth:

I eat and drink and piss and shit and sleep.

At work I breathe and do as I am told,

So I take no responsibility.

I take none, I don't, you may have it all.

I Feel More Like I Did When I Came in Here Than I Do Now

Jeff Mock

Sure, all roads lead round again to the heart,
But I'm lost in some far province—a toe
Or finger, peninsula—alone, hurt,
Sincere, and inconsequential. Each moment

I wake to strange sunrises, jollity
In a foreign tongue, air that smells of fish
And oil, grinding of sphinxian machinery
Down by the shore. There are no roads in this

Terra incognita. No petrol stations
To inquire directions. No maps for sale.
No rocks singing out advice. When I come
Upon starfish, they point five ways. Wee snails

Lumber down the beach, inch-by-inching outward.
The ocean rears up and back, gone and going.
Up in the hills, campfires blaze and the stars
Snap on. I hear everywhere some heart thumping.

Natural Habitats

Jeff Mock

Living Room:

Civilization began here, the first
Polite fuck on a ragged pelt.

I sip tea and read on, under
The electric light, of what came after:

Exhaustion, ah sadness, of course, and
The birth pains of the nations. The cur

Growls. I fall deeper into this book
Where the dead breathe comfortably.

The pendulum ticks off years. Torches
Flare. Four stone walls cave in on me.

Depot:

Rain, like a battered fedora,
Covers the horizon again. On board

The conductor ambles up and claims
Our next two tickets, and we start

Away from home after home. Our window

Passes from depot to desolation.

The locomotive was a crazy idea.
I wonder what I've left behind

That every station looks the same.
The tracks run together and depart.

Closet:

Each indiscretion is a bone locked
Therein, a misjoined skeleton—lovely,

Somehow—of too many nights and names.
Regret, the strongest ligament. The box

Of fidelity, carted from home to home,
Weighs less now and more on my mind.

In dreams the bones break together
Out and tease up beneath the sheets

And any name I let slip may well
Be right. It almost feels so fine.

South:

This lusty, floriferous countryside
Simply refuses to forget itself.

The days, the nights, the days!
Late last night, I devised an epic

Production of snow that lay
Like all the angels fallen, wings

Outspread, across the hills. I find,
This green morning, no such failing.

I wake to this: a heaven so perfect,
Alas, it pains both heart and mind.

Playroom:

Spring stuns the king's toys. All
The kings have theirs: an iron maiden,

Aye, the rack.—You see, he fits!—
Outside the kids howl and die like Christ,

Over and over. The older ones know how.
Slowly. Dramatically. A waterballoon

Decimates the neighbor's leisure.
He tumbles and dies well. That is it,

You see, to make each death so exquisite
That it must finally be pleasure.

Wilderness:

One must learn patience here
In the heart's ancient bedroom.

The great, murky wilds still arrive
Piece by piece, and every landscape

We ravage continues somehow to thrive.
Yes? By the bureau, yet another ax?

It may well take years to finally tame
One another. Yes? The alarm rings.

Some mornings are more than I dreamed
And some are sometimes much better.

Hummingbird

Jeff Mock

I

Hello, hummingbird, good morning, how are you?
Light from a far evening travels to meet you,
Light from a match, a candle, a city, light from the great
Metropolis of the Eastern seaboard. The light

Is on its way to you, my sweet needle on wings.
Do not fear. Do not fly away when the light
Approaches like a stranger. We are all strangers. Do not fear:
No stranger would stop to offer you the fresh

Poppy on his lapel. We are all friends, my needle, my dart,
My quick prick of conscience. The elm extends
Its branches to you, the garden cultivates its columbine
And firespike to nourish you, and this very evening

Someone will light a fire to show you the only way home.
Good morning, hummingbird, hello. The city buses
Dirty the air, the firehouse alarm shrills, the children
Are awake and well fed, and we all must leave like strangers.

II

I should not think of salvation, hummingbird, but I do.
I think it is painful. Some days we are eggshells, cracked open

And emptied. If our gods were more humane,
They would slink back to that original light and die

And leave us to the pain we cause ourselves and one
Another. Such pain we may have, all to our own, each so
Excruciatingly exquisite that we can only
Glory in it. Oh, my prick of conscience, let us dine

On the noxious weeds of the field. Let us dine
On the hollyhock, jewelweed, and fire pink the garden
Cultivates only for you. Let us dine on the passion
Of the wind that circles the earth. While you grow fat,

Let me dine on nothing human until I am at last
Nothing and may in time become human.
I may then think instead of the children who must be
Bathed, put to bed, woken, fed, and sent away like strangers.

                    III

Hummingbird, I've stored my heart in a coffer so I know
Where it is. Elsewise, I will forget it at the doctor's,
In a bus, under a flowering quince, in a stranger's bed. But we
Are all strangers, even I with my shoes spit-polished,

My slacks pressed, a dandelion pinned to my lapel, and dirt
Smudged on my left cheek. My hands are mud. Then
The light arrives. We gather in a meadow among
Sprays of touch-me-nots. Who would not make love

There among the thistles and nettles? Or glory in
A lungful of breath? Or wear her body as if it was tailored
To a T, her arms open to welcome, one by one,

Each other body, strangers all? Some days nectar flows

In our veins. We cannot contain it. We roll up our sleeves
And flex to pop that sweet vein. We extend our arms
To you, hummingbird. Strangers and friends, we fall to our knees
And cry out to you, *Take me, take me, drink of me.*

Bios

Forrest Aguirre lives and writes in Madison, Wisconsin. His work has appeared in such venues as *The Journal of Experimental Fiction, Exquisite Corpse, Asimovs*, and *Farrago's Wainscot;* and has been collected in *Fugue XXIX* (Raw Dog Screaming). He edited the anthology *Text:UR, The New Book of Masks* (Raw Dog Screaming) and *Polyphony 7* (Wheatland Press). He is a World Fantasy Award recipient for his editing, with Jeff VanderMeer, of *Leviathan 3* (Prime Books).

Forrest Armstrong is a writer from Boston, and the editor of this anthology. He is the author of the Wonderland Award-nominated *This City is Alive*, an art-novella done in collaboration with visual artist Jase Daniels. 2009 will see the release of his second and third books, *Asphalt Flowerhead* and *These Walls Don't Hold Out Space* (both from Crossing Chaos). Visit him at www.forrestarmstrong.com.

Steve Aylett is the author of 16 or so books including LINT, Slaughtermatic, Toxicology, And Your Point Is? and Shamanspace. He also does music, stand-up and comics such as 'Get That Thing Away From Me.' Though the story 'Gigantic' is nominally about 9/11, it was first published in 1998.

James Chapman has written eight novels, most recently *Degenerescence* and *How is This Going to Continue?* His work has appeared in *Word Riot, Prague Literary Review, Nth Position, Jacob's Ladder, Journal of Experimental Fiction, Dogmatika*, and others, as well as in a forthcoming anthology from Evil Nerd Empire Books. He lives in New York City with his wife, the novelist Randie Lipkin.

Amy Christmas lives in York, England. Her work has appeared in UK publications *Aesthetica, The Cadaverine, The Word* and *The Roundtable Review*.

Robert Chrysler is an inspired subway-ranter from Toronto, Canada. He enjoys challenging capitalist property relations, trying to figure out what the post-structuralists are going on about, and dreams of someday living in a tree. His work has appeared in: *Melancholia's Tremulous Dreadlocks, Venereal Kittens, Hammered Out, Van Gogh's Ear, Ditch PoetryThe Concelebratory ShoeHorn Review, The Guild of Outsider Writers*, and *The City Poetry*.

Jase Daniels was born in 1980. He is a mixed media artist, and has a degree in animation. He is currently recovering from a nasty flu virus and can't find the energy to put together a comprehensive biography, however he does have a website (www.jasedaniels.com) where you can see much more of his work and contact him directly if you want. Currently, when not flapping around in pools of his own bio-waste, he is hard at work on his first graphic novel *The Grubby End*, to be published by Crossing Chaos in 2009.

Kevin L. Donihe has had five books published via Eraserhead Press. His short fiction and poetry has appeared in *The Mammoth Book of Legal Thrillers, Flesh and Blood, ChiZine, The Cafe Irreal, Poe's Progeny, Book of Dark Wisdom, Dark Discoveries, Bathtub Gin, Not One of Us, Dreams and Nightmares, Electric Velocipede, Star*Line, Sick: An Anthology of Illness*, and other venues. He also edits the Bare Bone anthology series for Raw Dog Screaming Press, a story from which was reprinted in *The Mammoth Book of Best New Horror 13*. Visit him online at myspace.com/kevindonihe.

D. Grîn enjoys marmalade, riding his penny-farthing, and talking to the good folk who live in the tapioca clouds. He can often be found napping under a desk at the office of Crossing Chaos Enigmatic Ink.

C.J. Duffy died Easter Monday and the dust from his remains was scattered to be used as an organic compound. rather than select a root to be attached to, his creative force amalgamated with that of a rose bush; pretty but prickly. the bush grows out of Southern England not far from the southbank of London Town and at night emits a pungent scent.

Prakash Kona is an Indian novelist, essayist, poet and theorist who lives in Hyderabad, India. His books include *Pearls of an Unstrung Necklace* and *Streets that Smell of Dying Roses* published by Fugue State Press, New York. His areas of interest are pretty diverse ranging from politics to primroses to music and madness. Like all serious and not-so-serious writers he dreams of making a living through writing.

John Edward Lawson is an author and editor living near Washington, DC. He has published ten novels, fiction collections, illustrated books, and poetry collections. Hundreds of his works have appeared in publications around the world, most recently *National Lampoon's Animal House 29th Anniversary Edition, The Sound of Horror,* and *Masters of Unreality* (Germany). While serving as editor-in-chief of Raw Dog Screaming Press and *The Dream People* webzine, John has also edited six anthologies. In 2001 he was a winner of the Fiction International Emerging Writers Competition; in addition to being a Bram Stoker Award finalist other nominations include two for the Rhysling, two for the Dwarf Stars, and one for the Pushcart Prize.

Carlton Mellick III is the author of over twenty bizarro novels, including *The Menstruating Mall, Satan Burger, Haunted Vagina, The Baby Jesus Butt Plug, Ultra Fuckers,* and *The Egg Man,* among others. Check out his website at www.carltonmellick.com

Tim Miller's most recent book is The Lit World: Poems from History (S4N Books). He writes on religion and poetry at www.houseofthesun.org.

Jeff Mock is the author of *Evening Travelers,* a chapbook of poems published by Volans Press (1994), and *You Can Write Poetry,* a guide-book published by Writer's Digest Books (1998). His poems appear in *The Atlantic Monthly, Connecticut Review, The Georgia Review, The Iowa Review, New England Review, Quarterly West, The Sewanee Review, Shenandoah, The Southern Review,* and elsewhere. He teaches at Southern Connecticut State University.

John Moore-Williams is the author of the chapbook "I discover i is anandroid" (Trainwreck Press, 2008). His poetry and fiction have been published in *Shampoo, ditch, elimae, Venereal Kittens, Jack Magazine* and *Octaves,* among others. He looks forward to making the above publishing credits outdated by the time this book has released. In total agreement with William S. Burroughs that language is an extraterrestrial virus, he is feverishly engaged in the search for a vaccine.

murmurists is [Dr. A.L. Donovan]. British artist/musician. Born NW, 1963. Now Cafe Abdab, Mids. Eduheamosexual. Medium-build. Seeks similar. Yes, I have Yahoo; yes, I have MSN. (1) murmurists.blogspot.com (2) myspace.com/esoterian24skidoo

Joe L. Murr has lived on every habitable continent and currently resides in the Netherlands. His fiction has been published in *Read by Dawn I & II*, Dark Recesses Press and elsewhere.

Mike Philbin is the Oxford,UK-based author of several 'genreclectic' collections and novels including *Red Hedz* (1990), *Szmonhfu* (2001), *Animal Instincts* (2002), *Boyfistgirlsuck* (2003) and *Jane's Game* (2005). July 2008 saw the publication of two new novels from Silverthought Press of New York, *Bukkakeworld* and *Planet of the Owls*.

Cameron Pierce's fiction and poetry has appeared in Bare Bone, The Horror Library Vol. II, Bust Down the Door and Eat All the Chickens, Sein und Werden, and The Dream People, among other publications. His first book, Shark Hunting in Paradise Garden, is available from Eraserhead Press. Cameron currently lives in Olympia, WA.

Richard Polney is a graduate of the Clarion East Science Fiction Writing Workshop. His works have appeared in *Lady Churchill's Rosebud Wristlet*, and in the gay erotica anthologies *Wet Dream—Wet Nightmares, Men on the Edge*, and *Taken by Force*. Contrary to what many people are saying, Rick isn't dead. As a matter of fact, he's not even close.

Lynn Strongin   Born and raised in the Northeast and deep South during WWII, Lynn Strongin has twelve books published, and is a five-time Pushcart Prize nominee. Her anthology *The Sorrow Psalms* "A Book of Twentieth-Century Elegy" was a best seller in England. Its companion volume *Crazed by the sun*, "Poems of Ecstasy" will be published this summer by Cyberwit.Net (The academic publisher.) Her forthcoming books are *Cape Seventy* (a book of poems on a woman contemplating turning seventy, a poet) and *Albino Peacock* (Short stories of a Southern Jewish childhood) as well as the memoir *Indigo*. The memoir and book of poems will be published by Thorp Stprings Press, Austin and will be available over Amazon.com. *Albino Peacock* will also be available over Amazon and is being published in autumn 2008 by Plain View Press, Austin.

Kek-W   Land-locked deep in the dark, mythic heart of England's West County, **Kek-w** is Somerset's own twisted renaissance man. A music critic and alt.culture obsessive, he writes regularly for UK magazines such *FACT, Dazed & Confused* and *Woofah*, as well as *Groove* magazine in Germany. He has written comic-scripts for the weekly UK comic 2000AD and is one half of the psychedelic-surrealist music-collective Ice Bird Spiral.

He has had short stories published in various *Nemonymous*, *Crossing Chaos*, *Read by Dawn* and *Chimeraworld* anthologies, as well as *The Dream People* e-magazine. Assorted pieces of experimental prose fiction and art have appeared on the *Venereal Kittens*, *Otoliths* and *Starfish Journal* websites. His story "Blue Raspberries" was nominated for the *Best Short Fiction of 2007* award by the BSFA (British Science Fiction Association).

D.D.Wildblood is a writer and illustrator from Yorkshire, England.

Thomas Wiloch has published several collections of prose poems, including *Tales of Lord Shantih*, *Screaming in Code*, *Stigmata Junction*, and *Mr. Templeton's Toyshop*. He also has work in *Double Room*, *Star*Line*, *Big Toe Review*, *MicroHorror*, and *Flashshot*.

Stephen M. Wilson is poetry editor for *Doorways Magazine* and co editor (w/Deborah P Kolodji) of the Dwarf Stars Award anthology. His work has been nominated for six Rhysling Awards and a Gaylactic Spectrum Award and received an honorable mention from Ellen Datlow in *Year's Best Fantasy and Horror 19*. Stephen lives in California.

Kristopher Young lives in Portland, Oregon. He is the author of *Click* and one of the minds behind Another Sky Press, a radical publishing company that does things a little differently. He is currently working on many projects, one of which may just be his next novel.

Books from Raw Dog Screaming Press

Blankety Blank, D. Harlan Wilson
hc 978-1-933293-50-9, $14.95, 188p
tpb 978-1-933293-57-8, $29.95, 188p

Rutger Van Trout has problems but the worst is not that his son might be a werewolf. It's not his obsession with transforming his house into a three-ring barnyard or his wife's haunted skeleton. The complication has invaded his community in the form of a new breed of serial killer, who stalks from house to house leaving a bloodbath that would make Jack the Ripper himself blush.

Isabel Burning, Donna Lynch
hc 978-1-933293-49-3, $29.95, 236p
tpb 978-1-933293-56-1, $15.95, 236p

Isabel's new job as housekeeper at Grace mansion allows her to observe the habits of the enigmatic Dr. Edward Grace. Captivated by his tales of travel to Africa, she is inexorably drawn into a tumultuous relationship which eventually reveals the Grace family's dark heritage and lays bare every secret, even the ones she keeps from herself.

Sin Conductor, John Edward Lawson
tpb 978-1-933293-65-3

Willis Lowery is just your average occupational hazards estimator until one day, while inspecting a factory, he happens across a chemical burn victim. Her name is Dusyanna, and the passion she ignites in him threatens to melt away every fiber of his morals. As he soon learns, there is no escape from her circle of degenerates, so he vows to become the devil to beat the devil.

Jesus Coyote Harold Jaffe
hc 978-1-933293-55-4, $24.95, 148p
tpb 978-1-933293-63-9, $13.95, 148p

This docufictional novel based on the Manson murders proves that, like his coyote totem, the myths around Manson hold irrevocable power. In one swooping panoramic arc, with the bloody killings at its center, Jaffe captures the perspectives of Manson, his devotees, the prosecutors, and the victims while firing a shot against the hypocrisy of institutionalized morality.

www.rawdogscreaming.com

Books from Raw Dog Screaming Press

Lowlife Underdogs, Dustin LaValley
tpb 978-1-933293-64-6, $14.95, 200p
Bouts of brutality spark a flash of recognition, a reminder of younger years when we were bullied apathetically by teachers, bosses and peers. In those moments LaValley transforms lowlifes into underdogs who, though seriously misguided, never stop fighting

Worse Than Myself, Adam Golaski
hc 978-1-933293-66-0, $29.95, 216p
tpb 978-1-933293-67-7, $29.95, 216p

A successor to Lovecraft, Adam Golaski spins dark, weird tales in the original sense of the word: uncanny, unearthly, sometimes fantastic and always slightly off center. These are stories to be savored late at night in bed read by the light of a single lamp in an empty, dark house.

Lemur, Tom Bradley
hc 978-1-933293-54-7, $22.95, 120p
tpb 978-1-933293-61-5, $11.95, 120p

Spencer Sproul longs to follow in the footsteps of his heros: Ted Bundy and John Wayne Gacy. Who wouldn't be murderous stuck in a restaurant with an asshole boss, sadistic co-workers and Lemmy the Lemur as a mascot? But he doesn't have a killer's instinct. However, Spencer soon learns that a family restaurant can be an instrument of torture and quickly becomes a rising star in the food service industry

Health Agent, Jeffrey Thomas
hc 978-1-933293-43-1, $30.00, 228p
tpb 978-1-933293-44-8, $15.95, 228p

When performance art starts infecting citizens of Punktown with an untreatable illness health agent Monty Black is assigned to investigate. But the situation is even more serious than it seems and he gets tangled up in an evil scheme that threatens to tear the city apart.

www.rawdogscreaming.com